For my own Mr Scott,

Your faith in me lent me the strength I needed until
I rediscovered it within myself.

Your Tiny

# TALISMANS, TEACUPS & TRYSTS

## K. STARLING

Copyright © 2024 Kendra Dyson

ISBN (paperback): 979-8-9906466-0-5
ISBN (ebook): 979-8-9906466-1-2

Dragon silhouettes by Freepik.com

www.authorkstarling.com

First Edition: July 2024

# CHAPTERS TITLES

# Narrator's Note

Dearest Reader,

We are about to embark on a whimsical adventure.
First, though, I must warn you:

This tale contains frivolity, mischief,
*and* mayhem.

It also contains harm to animals, bullying, and
murder; however, as this is a cosy tale, such things
take place off-page.

Oh! And there are brawls

Consider yourself forewarned.

P.S. You may spot what *you* believe are historical
inaccuracies in this story. In our universe, dragons
beg for scraps at the dinner table, and unicorns
occasionally bless babes at their christening. In
other words, things are a tad different in our world.
Keep calm and carry on.

# CHARACTERS OF NOTE

(and a few less noteworthy ones)

PENELOPE SEDGEWICK ∘ Our heroine

VERITY WALTERS (Walt, if you please) ∘ Assistant and spoon aficionado

UNCLE ARCHIE ∘ Uncle to Penelope and mad scientist

AUNT JOSEPHINE ∘ Aunt to Penelope and sister to Archie

TOAST ∘ A forest dragon and friend

MRS STEVENSON ∘ Aunt Josephine's dearest friend

AMBROSE ∘ A miniature zilant dragon and friend to Aunt Josephine

CERBERUS ∘ A faedragon (not a three-headed dog) and friend to Uncle Archie

SABLE (Not Miss or Mistress) ∘ A nurturer and a healer

MR BEN SCOTT, THE YETI ∘ Not what you would expect

VISCOUNTESS MONTAGU ∘ Aunt to Mr Montagu

FRANK THE FOOTMAN ∘ A scrumptious flirt, and footman to the Pilkingtons

GRACE SULLIVAN ∘ A maid and secret lover to . . . ?

JAMES SULLIVAN ∘ Brother to Grace

MRS BATES ∘ The Pilkingtons' housekeeper

MR TOBIAS MONTAGU ∘ A would-be viscount

MISS ROSE PILKINGTON ∘ The tryster

LADY PILKINGTON ∘ Mother of the tryster

SIR LAWRENCE PILKINGTON ∘ Father of the tryster

MR U ∘ A curate whose name is still unknown

MISS HARRIET GREENE ∘ A loquacious young lady

HIS LORDSHIP, THE EARL OF ALDERWOOD ∘ Uncle Archie's archnemesis and best friend

GOOD OLE FRANNY ∘ He will keep

# CHAPTER 1

## The Chapter that Begins It All

"Historians believe that, had dragons not been domesticated in the early half of the 17th century, feathers rather than scales would have prevailed as the embellishment of choice in the fashionable world."

*On the Trade of Dragon Scales, Claws, Venom, and Teeth in Britain and the Americas, page 137*

When Penelope Sedgewick set out that morning, she did not expect to spend her afternoon wedged behind a cart of dragon dung. However, since she was determined to report on the movements of her client's future son-in-law, she assumed an unladylike squat and waited. After around a quarter of an hour, when her left foot had lost sensation and was begging her to stand, he appeared—Sir Charles, a baronet, affianced to an influential tradesman's daughter.

To call him a dandy might have been impolite, and yet to call him otherwise would be a lie. It was his lurid suit—with more flourishes than ought to be permitted on one man's coat—that first caught her attention. Through the crack in the stall door, she spied his expression. Any mother, parson, or judge would be familiar with that look, the one worn by guilty men and mischievous children alike.

For one week, she had trailed him, and she had yet to ascertain the precise nature of his furtive meetings. Raucous laughter had foiled her attempts to overhear his conversation at the pub two evenings prior. While her disguise as a sleeping traveller had protected her from the wandering eyes (and hands) of the patrons, it had not permitted her to move near Sir Charles without drawing his attention.

Gaining entry to the gentlemen's club had been simple enough. With her petite frame, pert nose, and lively hazel eyes, she could pass for a pixie-like boy of fourteen or fifteen easily enough. Unfortunately, an earl had sent her from the room to seek the evening paper—an errand she completed so as not to have her ears boxed.

Today would be the day; of that, she was certain. She had found the date, time, and location scribbled on a scrap of paper in his pocket. (How she extracted it from his pocket and returned it without him the wiser is a story for another time, though rumour had it that the baronet blushed during the encounter, as did his footman.) A true professional, she had disguised herself as an errand boy and secreted herself in the stable while the coachman had been occupied wrangling an amethyst dragon who had "got loose" in the west field.

The coachman, hired for his pleasing appearance, welcomed Sir Charles with a greeting so loud that centuries of dust were shaken from the rough-hewn rafters onto her face, nearly soliciting a sneeze. Thankfully, her twenty-seven years of training as a lady had given her the self-possession required not to burst forth with a resounding "Achoo!"

Through the crack in the stable door, she observed the gentleman's scowl. The expression heightened the severity of his sharp features. "Do be quiet!"

Penelope's heart-shaped lip curled in disgust as she shuffled through what she decided was water mixed with straw (though her nose told her otherwise) to get a better view of the pair. Whitewashed bricks reflected what little light the overcast day could muster. The pale glow filtered through the windows, highlighting the well-swept stone floor. Across from her, an indigo-coloured dragon slept; its gauzy wings were curled over its face. Thankfully, neither the dragon nor a pair of chestnut trotters in the neighbouring stall were disturbed by her presence.

"Forgive me, sir." Although the coachman's tone indicated that he was far from apologetic, his remark placated the gentleman, who waved him to his polished black phaeton drawn by a pair of black ponies. "Lord! Where'd you find 'em, if you don't mind me asking?"

His lip pulled into a sneer. "As it happens, I do mind."

"Stolen, weren't they?"

The "they" in question was unclear to Penelope, though she had her suspicions. As Alderwood bordered the Forest of Dean, it had become famous (if not infamous) for the trade of certain artefacts. While the steady stream of adventure seekers hoping to glimpse a yeti or an Irish elk kept the tradesmen's children in new shoes, the locals found whispered requests for talismans or referrals to practitioners of certain illicit arts tedious. Though she was unsure what his cart contained, she was certain that it was valuable.

"They were not," bit back the baronet. "Actually, these came from my estate."

"If you have one of those, why not sell it instead?"

Penelope had patience—mountains of it, in fact. Still, the men's lack of specificity was wearing it thin.

"Sell? A silver dragon? Clearly, you know nothing about the patronage of dragons."

*Clearly.* She pressed her lips together, suppressing a smirk. Dragon scales. Of course. She had guessed as much.

The baronet, entitled man that he was, interrupted her silent celebration by lifting a wooden crate from its compartment under the seat of the low-slung, four-wheeled carriage. As he did, the burlap cloth covering the spoils slipped. Sunlight caught the corner of the glassy scales, reflecting a blast of silvery hues across her face. Instinctively, she recoiled.

A scene of a vast cerulean expanse flashed through her mind's eye. Tufts of clouds drifted in the distance. Penelope felt a welcome weightlessness—as though her cares had remained on earth while her spirit took flight. She inhaled deeply.

Though she wished to linger in the vision, soaking in the remnants of the dragon's memory imbued in its scales, she fluttered her dark lashes. She was a professional and had a job to do. No time to dilly-dally.

Her momentary vision had distracted her from the task at hand. (Blast!) She had missed Sir Charles's response, only catching the other man's retort. "Keep your hat on. I couldn't care less how you got 'em, so long as there was nothing sordid about it."

The baronet's expression communicated that his dealings with dragons were anything but sordid. Occupied with inspecting and counting the scales—several dozen by Penelope's estimation—the coachman conveniently missed his scowl.

Finally, he withdrew a cotton purse from his pocket. He tossed it unceremoniously to the gentleman, who nearly dropped it.

A cursory glance at its contents solicited a genuine smile, which Sir Lawrence quickly shoved aside. It was an unspoken rule among certain men of substance that grins were to be reserved for poorly told jokes and naughty limericks.

With the purse safely stowed in his pocket, he stepped towards the door. A drizzle had begun to pepper the windows with watery freckles. Doubtless, he wished to be on his way before the weather worsened. "Whatever will the scales be used for?"

A thrust of the coachman's chin directed their gazes to an imposing carriage at the opposite end of the stables. "To adorn her ladyship's private coach."

When Penelope eyed the green scales covering the lower half of the vehicle, painted a lush peacock blue, the word ostentatious came to mind. Every inch of it had been polished to a high sheen, which, on the odd sunny day, would have blinded pedestrians.

The gentleman climbed into his phaeton, taking the reins in hand. "She has enemies, I take it."

"One or two." The coachman shrugged. "But the scales will do more to inflate her ladyship's vanity than protect her person."

With a snap of the reins, the gentleman departed—not a moment too soon, as Penelope's right foot threatened to join her left one in becoming as limp as an overcooked carrot.

Unfortunately, rather than scurry to her ladyship with his spoils in tow, the coachman fawned over the teardrop-shaped scales, humming to himself as he admired them one by one (and may have slipped one into his pocket, but you did not hear that from me).

It was her policy to shoot only when threatened. She generally succeeded with the aid of a judicious amount of tea and patience; however, as squatting for a sustained period had caused her . . . well, shall we say aft to burn, she considered making an exception.

{Narrator Note: Dearest Reader, a scandalous rumour has spread that our heroine did, in fact, shoot at the coachman later that evening. She did not. That he was a party to an incident involving pistols and drink that same day is neither here nor there. Besides, had she been involved, she would not have missed.}

The heavens must have disapproved of her musings, for they intervened. While she envisioned herself quietly drawing her weapon from her oversized wool coat, the fortunate servant lifted the crate and departed.

No sooner had his tread faded than she rose to her feet, gripping a beam for support. She did not exhale a sigh of relief, nor did she wipe her brow—ladies did not sweat. Instead, she waited for the tingling to cease before she stole through a rear door, nodded at two passing gardeners, and vanished into the forest.

# CHAPTER 2

## The Chapter with the Lust

*"Brevity is the soul of a well-written chapter"*

*An Anonymous Narrator*

Three hours, a cup of tea, and a change of clothing later, she arrived at the doorstep of her client disguised as Prudence Clearwater, a lady secretary she had invented to carry out business on her behalf without divulging her true identity.

Unlike Penelope, Prudence was a shy yet capable woman with owl-like spectacles, bushy black eyebrows, and a pursed mouth, perpetually prepared to whisper. The charm she wore not only tripled her eyebrows' thickness but dulled her naturally clear skin as well. Her dress was plain, made of striped cotton paired with a grey wool waist-length coat. To sell the part, she had even studied the accent of the West Country, emphasising her rhotic Rs and dropping her Ts with glee. It fitted Prudence's imagined provincial upbringing nicely.

As she was shown into the drawing room, she adjusted her straw bonnet, reminding herself to lower her chin. Secretaries ought not to appear ascendant.

A haughty woman with enough neck for two ladies (ideal for nosing about in the business of others) gestured to a wingback chair, indicating that Penelope ought to be seated. Her client—like her hall, her servants, and her drawing room—could be summarised in one word: gaudy. The vulgar colour palette (that reminded her of vomit) and the clashing patterns made Penelope feel sick. As she took her seat, she could not decide which she detested most, the putrid floral drapes or the cherry-hued rug.

The footman (whose breeches did not match his coat) had hardly closed the door before the lady spoke. "Is my future son-in-law a rake or a gambler?"

"Neither, madam. He is not even a drunkard or a coffee drinker." Penelope's voice barely rose above a whisper. She clasped her gloved hands in her lap, keeping her head bent.

The matron rolled her watery eyes. "Rather dull, is he not?"

Prudence did not chuckle, though internally, Penelope did. "I am afraid so."

"What is he then?"

Penelope's heart leapt in her chest. These were the moments that made the sleepless nights and frigid hours spent out of doors in the rain worth it. No, she lived a double life not for the money (pocket change) or the prestige, but for the look that dawned in the eyes of her clients when they understood all that she had discovered.

She willed the tremor in her core to quiet before she spoke. "A young man in love, intent on modernising his estate. His late evenings and frequent journeys have been in the pursuit of customers in the market for scales."

Her client nodded and sipped from a teacup that monstrous pickle and gold embellishments had ruined. She had neglected to offer a cup to Penelope. Though this was not a social call, such behaviour was considered rude by polite society. However, what could she expect? Her client was one of those "nouveaux riches" and had yet to learn the customs kept by the upper crust.

"There are worse things to be, I suppose." She waved her hand, nearly blinding Penelope with the baubles that encrusted her fingers and wrist.

Our heroine took care to exaggerate her blinks in such a way that conveyed confusion. "Than what, ma'am?"

"A man who deals in the illicit trade of magical items." She savoured a second sip. "It almost makes him interesting."

"Unfortunately, he is not." The corner of Prudence's coral lip did not lift, not even a hairbreadth. "He patrons the dragon in question and came by the scales legally."

Given how the lady's eye flashed and her lips pursed, one would have thought she had learnt something seductively salacious about Sir Charles. "He patrons a dragon, you say?"

Leaning in, Prudence whispered, "A silver."

"I see." Her lips parted in wonderment. No doubt visions of her grandchildren inheriting an estate that was home to a dragon (a flailing estate in desperate need of capital, but a prestigious one, nonetheless) were flitting through her mind.

Penelope reclined against the richly upholstered canapé. Externally, she appeared collected, whilst internally, she did a complicated series of acrobatics.

Two five-pound notes were withdrawn from a nearby book and extended to Penelope, who accepted them with due deference. As she and the client had agreed upon less for the information provided, her generosity betrayed her satisfaction. "Thank your mistress for her time. Please tell her I am very pleased with her thoroughness."

She accepted the notes, stowing them in her pocket. Penelope's actual assistant (with whom she split her earnings fifty-fifty) would be pleased, as would the director of the local school for girls when her half of the sum was delivered anonymously. "It was her pleasure, ma'am."

{Narrator's Note: Though dressmakers, in their infinite wisdom, had declared pockets as gauche, our heroine believed they were sensible and, therefore, essential. Her dressmaker had expertly secreted two in her dress and one in her waist-length spencer, using a concealment charm to disguise them.

What they contained is a matter for another day, and whether the wyvern feather in her bonnet was actually a petite dagger is none of our concern.}

With that, she bowed, rose, and crossed the room to depart. Before her hand had grasped the knob, her client called, "A silver, you say?"

Penelope did not turn. To turn would ruin the dramatic effect and reveal the satisfaction that danced in her hazel eyes. "For four generations."

As she passed through the door, she could have sworn she heard the lady chuckle with delight.

# CHAPTER 3

## The Chapter with the Loquacious Maid

"Adults shall be permitted to carry no more than
three talismans on their person at once. Children
may carry one, unless their physician recommends
a second to remedy a persistent malady. Exceptions
may be granted by the local governing body on
holidays."

*The Law Governing Magic and Magickind, 1798*

Plainness was a mantle Penelope wore gladly, especially as
it permitted her to go unnoticed by flirts and busybodies
alike. This was why she remained attired in the sensible
dress and plain poke bonnet of Prudence Clearwater as
she weaved through the streets of Alderwood.

A vase of flowers had been placed in the window of
her actual assistant's home that morning—the agreed-
upon sign that a message had been received. Hence, she
was resolved to stop by. First, though, she would take pains
to overhear a titbit of gossip and exchange a halfpenny or
two for information from a handful of reliable purveyors
of whispered information.

The streets of Alderwood teemed with the vibrant hum of trade and tourism. Rows of limestone and red-brick buildings lined the thoroughfare, their colourful yellow and red shutters defying the drizzle that had descended on the town. Wooden signs and placards advertising reputable dowsers and experienced milliners jutted into the narrower lanes, a hazard to gentlemen's hats. Flower baskets hung from hooks near the doorways as if to welcome spring and its sunnier weather. All in all, it was a picturesque town, just as the advertisements promised.

As her usual haunts were dull, void of any scintillating gossip or even a humorous riddle, Penelope sought to soothe her disappointment by pausing at a cart to purchase a bag of sugared blueberries—a treat for both ladies and dragons alike, or so said the placard.

A halfpenny poorer, she was about to turn towards her offices when her eye caught a familiar face, one that had the potential to make her trip into the heart of Alderwood worthwhile. There, opposite her, beyond the dragon-drawn carriages and pairs of ladies clustered under black umbrellas carefully avoiding the puddles, stood the local physician's housemaid, Miss Harriet Greene. Penelope quickened her pace to intercept the girl, who possessed a loose tongue and a passion for fine clothes.

Careful to avoid the spray from passing carriage wheels and dragon droppings littering her path, she cut across the cobblestone street. She kept her eye locked on the faux canary-yellow scales that adorned the maid's bonnet as it bobbed and weaved through the crowd. With an impressive display of nimble footwork, Penelope gained the opposite corner—unrumpled and not winded in the least—at the same instant as Miss Greene.

The maid's eyes lit up like a candelabrum when she caught sight of Prudence (who did not smile nor preen at her good fortune). After pleasantries were exchanged, Miss Greene, a short girl of nineteen with a smattering of freckles across her nose, leaned in close. "The doctor was called to the field this morning. Paid well, I hear."

A rude fellow shoved betwixt them carrying a sign reading, "Folk are Vermin. Reverse the Magic Act." in lurid red lettering. Penelope caught his eye, and by the way he fled, it was safe to presume she had unleashed upon him the Sedgewick Stare.

{Narrator's Note: If you are not familiar with the Sedgewick Stare, permit me to describe it. Imagine a goddess in the form of a hydra who ate her enemies for breakfast and used their bones to pick her teeth. Now imagine her grandmother and the look she would give her wayward grandchild. The Sedgewick Stare is reportedly more frightening than that.}

The ladies stepped to one side, eager to avoid further interruptions. "Did you happen to overhear who called for his services?"

"Not exactly, but that the duel was between a gentleman and farmer. Good man, level-headed, he said—the farmer, not the gentleman." A passing officer dressed in regimentals caught the maid's eye. Her cheeks shaded crimson as she tried and failed to disguise her pleasure.

When a half guinea was withdrawn from the pocket of Penelope's skirt, the girl tore her chestnut eyes from the officer. "He said the farmer was wounded. Nothing serious. Says he should recover quickly. Can try to find out their names if you like."

They bade their farewells. Penelope categorised the information in her mind somewhere between scone recipes and rhinological terms before turning her tread to the busiest corner in all of Alderwood.

While those who work in secret often prefer remote locations for their offices, if you are a lady who surreptitiously investigates matters for other ladies, the ideal location for said offices is on a busy thoroughfare between a hat shop and a dressmaker. Such a location permitted her clients to come and go without suspicion. After all, well-meaning (in other words, bothersome) gentlemen become concerned when their wives or daughters traipse through the woods, yet think nothing of them paying a visit to the local herbalist to procure a salve for acne or a cure for a blighted love life.

When she stood on the corner opposite her offices, she spied the vase through the wavy glass window. The half-timbered style of the building, with its exposed, blackened frame and white plaster walls, was quaint enough to draw a tourist's eye, and respectable enough to solicit more than a passing glance. Its thatched roof disguised it as a thoroughly Elizabethan structure rather than the modern building it was— intentionally constructed to appear centuries older.

The herbalist's shop, through which she had to pass to gain access to her assistant's rooms, was a beehive of activity. With the Season approaching, every woman in the county had descended on the town to order dresses or purchase beauty creams.

As she stepped through the door, the odour of a hundred varieties of herbs and spices bombarded her senses. Honey-coloured wooden shelves were lined with neat rows of jars and boxes containing all manner of cures and restoratives. This was no cramped cavern with faint lighting or a smoking chimney. Cecilia's Cabinet was a proper establishment, complete with swept floors, polished windows, and proper lighting. Everything from its spotless shelves to the crisp linen aprons worn by the shopkeeper's assistants screamed respectability. Nothing like those back-alley cures peddled elsewhere, thank you very much.

As she approached a matronly woman with a daughter fawning over rouge, Penelope's nose twitched—the telltale sign that one of them wore a charm.

"Oh, mama, which should I choose?"

"Not that one." The dear mama snatched the jar from her hand. "You are trying to attract a husband, not the unwanted attention of a rake."

The glimmer that flashed in the young woman's eyes convinced Penelope that the attentions of a rake would not be rebuffed and that she might, in fact, welcome them enthusiastically.

The pressing need to sneeze caused Penelope to hasten her pace. However, it was not the dear mama who bore the charm but her daughter, for when Penelope drew nearer to the pair, she could sense it—a tug of sorts, accompanied by the scent of honeysuckles. She dodged them by turning down an aisle containing cures for rheumatism and baldness.

Thankfully, she encountered only one other talisman, two faint smiles, and one squashed toe before she gained the back hall. While the six doors that lined the corridor appeared to enclose six private consultation rooms, one door led, instead, to a stairwell. It was through this door that Penelope passed, ignoring the wooden placard that read, "Please do not disturb."

This was no typical stairwell; it bore no shoe scuffs or smudged hand prints. The polished wood framing gleamed, and the white walls shone as though they had been painted yesterday. At the upper landing, she passed the door that led to her observation chamber, a narrow room that permitted her to scrutinise clients without their knowledge.

It was the second door she opened, the one that bore a gleaming metal placard that read, "Mrs Patience Jones. Please knock." As she entered the room, it was not Mrs Patience Jones who lounged across a sage wingback chair, puffing on a pipe. If Mrs Jones had been present, Penelope would have thought she was going mad, for monikers and figments of one's imagination cannot come to call (or, at least, they should not).

No, it was her assistant, Miss Verity Walters, or Walt, as she had insisted on being called since her third birthday. She held an unlit pipe, worn at the bowl by frequent use, in one hand and the morning paper in the other. Still dressed in her bottle-green robe with her coiled curls tumbling down her shoulders, she lounged like a Greek goddess being fanned by a palm leaf.

Penelope did not let her lip curl in disgust as she observed that the corners of the paper were soiled with oily fingerprints, the result of a midday snack of cold meats. "I see that you have had a productive day."

{Narrator's Note: Reader, she had not had a productive day.}

"Indeed I have." As it was merely her employer and not a client, Walt took no pains to disguise her rustic drawl. She laid her paper aside. "I've done a good deal while you've been flitting about."

Penelope crossed to her desk, which stood near the window overlooking the main road. Like the rest of the room, it reflected her personality—timeless elegance with a hint of mischievousness lurking in the shadows. Her desk was tidy, with her letters stacked in neat piles and her quill and letter opener lying parallel.

The robin-egg blue walls, trimmed with white moulding, had tales of their own to tell. Visitors, for instance, often overlooked the ghost added to the oil painting of an idyllic country scene. They also missed the dagger under the tea cart or the sword masquerading as a walking stick.

No one knew of the compartment in the desk that hid a stash of fine chocolates, not even Walt. And few suspected that a floral tapestry hid a target at which she often threw knives or fired arrows. The ghost had been added because it was amusing, whereas the rest were practical. After all, where else could an heiress practice knife-throwing or store her small sword?

19

Once the door had been closed and locked, Penelope shed her locket—one that cleverly hid a coiffure charm—ridding her of the bushy eyebrows and a faint compulsion to sneeze. It was the ideal disguise, for if a sniffer were to sense the talisman, they would safely assume she wore it to enhance her luxuriant sable hair, which was her finest feature, rather than to transform her eyebrows into overgrown hedges.

Before assuming her seat, she paused to smooth her hair. As the mirror had been hung at Walt's eyeline, she had to stand on her tip-toes.

Her maid had coaxed her wavy hair into an elegant bun befitting her station. A few loose tendrils framed her impish face. If she were not to inherit an estate worth thousands per annum, society would have admonished her appearance, labelling it as fae-like with her pointy chin and upturned button nose. However, when one's family owns a quarter of the countryside, society tends to categorise such faults as "pretty" or "childlike" instead.

"Thank the Heavens!" interjected Walt as she lit her pipe. "Whenever you wear that thing, I can barely control myself. I'm afeared that one day, I'll burst into laughter. That or smack the woolly caterpillars off your face."

"I would prefer neither." Penelope selected her preferred cup and saucer, a light blue Wedgewood with white florals, her mother's, before settling into her chair. "They are a bit over the top, but they disguise my identity well; however, I could go back to the woman I acquired it from and ask her to adjust the talisman if you find it too distracting. It would lower our profits by a few pounds, but . . ."

Walt filled her employer's cup with freshly brewed tea, leaving ample room to stir in honey. "Nah, no need. Self-control is the hallmark of my trade."

Self-control was not an adjective Penelope would have assigned to her assistant. Walt smoked her pipe incessantly, purchased more fine watches than she ought, went to the theatre entirely too often, and had a proclivity for stealing teaspoons, which her employer never expressly permitted nor took pains to put an end to.

Both women settled into their chairs. A comfortable silence enfolded them. While they were technically employer and employee, in reality they were confidantes and partners. Without Penelope, Walt would not have escaped the theatre to become a gainfully employed, respectable woman. (Nor would she have been alive, but that is a story for another day.) Without Walt, Penelope would not have been able to continue to wear the mask of Miss Sedgewick, heiress, while flexing her intellect by solving mysteries. The arrangement was mutually beneficial. The one gained enough money to keep her in tobacco and cakes, and the other gained an opportunity to challenge her mind.

"A letter has arrived, I take it." Penelope eyed an envelope on the mantel.

"Indeed." Walt's caramel-coloured eyes remained trained on her paper, unwilling to admit that she had failed to place the note on its specified spot. Her employer had even purchased a pricey piece of Limoges china to receive letters.

An imperceptible tut from her employer drove Walt to her feet. With a feigned formality that Penelope did not condone yet secretly found delightful, the letter was delivered.

"Thank you."

*Miss Jones,*
*If you would do me the honour of presenting yourself*
*at the Abbey at your earliest convenience to discuss a*
*matter of some import. Please request Lady Pilkington.*
*A.P.*

"Another request?"

"Yes." She folded the letter before handing it to Walt. "From Lady Pilkington."

"Her husband's got more acres than hairs on his head, hasn't he?"

"Do not most men?" Penelope closed her eyes, memorizing the letter. "Even the poor ones."

Of course, she and Lady Pilkington were acquaintances. Lady Pilkington had a daughter near Penelope's age, so they crossed paths often enough. Though they would never be friends, they were on good terms. She relished the prospect of taking on this matter; to deceive an acquaintance would be a testament to her prowess as an investigator.

"Not much to go on." The letter was returned to the plate.

"There never is." Penelope tugged at a curl of her fine hair, wrapping it and unwrapping it around her finger while yanking memories and catalogued rumours concerning the family from the recesses of her mind. "When can you be ready?"

"In a quarter of an hour."

"Meet me in two hours, then." She rose and crossed to the bedchamber, where she had stowed her everyday clothes. "I am due for my afternoon stroll."

As she stepped behind the screen to transform herself into an heiress once more, Walt called out, "Should I bring my pistol, or will my knife suffice?"

Penelope did not grin . . . well, maybe a little. "My dear, a pistol is as essential to a lady's ensemble as stockings. Never leave home without one."

# CHAPTER 4

## The Chapter with the Sir Loon

"The existence of the Beast of Bodmin Moor
has been recorded throughout the annals of British
history since 1512; however, it was not until 1796 that
scientists confirmed that the beast was, in fact, the
offspring of a sabre-toothed tiger and a house cat."

*Cryptozoology in Modern England, Wales,
and Scotland, Fourth Edition, Page 112*

Birch Hallow was precisely the sort of home three geniuses with peculiar personalities would inhabit. Thankfully, three such persons were born to it—Penelope, her aunt, and her uncle. The coincidence was such that the neighbourhood had speculated as to whether the house was imbued with magic so potent it transformed its occupants into oddities.

It bore a resemblance to a fine manor, with limestone bricks, shale shingles, and an appropriate number of well-trimmed hedges. However, upon further examination, guests often discovered trebuchets in the garden and spare body parts in jars on the windowsills. Once, the parson swore he had spotted the Beast of Bodmin Moor near the pond. Whether said beast had or had not resided at Birch Hallow is of no import; after all, ladies kept dragons as house pets.

What did matter was that our fair heroine had arrived home, dressed as an heiress rather than as a secretary.

{Narrator's Note: As readers have expressed concern regarding the aforementioned body parts, rest assured, all the pickled appendages and whatnots were properly stored and had been obtained legally (mostly).}

After leafing through the heap of correspondence that had accumulated in her absence and finding that it chiefly contained invitations to social events (Drat!) or cards from the mothers of desperate would-be suitors inviting her to tea (Double drat!), Penelope sought refuge in the garden and, she hoped, her uncle's company.

Uncle Archibald, or Uncle Archie as she called him when not in the presence of her aunt, stood amidst the roses. As per usual, his entire person rebelled against order—frizzed salt-and-pepper hair, watches dangling from every available pocket, and a rumpled suit. Despite his valet's best efforts, Archie's suits resisted orderliness. The moment they touched his skin, they began to wrinkle of their own accord.

A twinkle bright enough to dwarf the noon-day sun lit up his features. Silently, he signed, "Good afternoon, Penny. Fine day, is it not?"

She eyed the overcast sky with windows of blue here and there. "It is lovely, now that the rain has cleared. And have you managed to avoid making much mischief this morning?"

"Of course not. It is my duty as the resident loon to make as much mischief as possible." A nod of his head directed their steps towards a sheltered maze they frequented in the afternoon.

"Hmm. I had always heard people call you eccentric." She considered him. "Loon suits, I suppose."

Her hands formed the words fluently, for she had learned them alongside spoken English. Even though her parents could hear, her uncle could not, and he had resided with them since her infancy. Hence, she had been raised learning English, sign language, Greek, and Latin. She dabbled in French, German, Flemish, Gaelic, and Spanish, but only for fun.

"It has been six months since the town began to address me as 'Sir Loon.' Or so the cook has told me."

"Then you will sign your letters . . ." She sneaked a knowing glance at her uncle. ". . . by 'Sir Loon' beginning next Sunday, I presume."

When dear Uncle Archie answered with a naughty hand gesture, Penelope pressed her hand to her chest. Though her wide hazel eyes insinuated shock, in reality she was tickled. She did love contrariness.

A peck on his stubbled cheek smoothed his ruffled scales. "Just as well. Your reputation as the village madman shields us from hosting two balls a year."

The pair sneered. Balls. Ugh!

"Is it not sufficient torture that we should be forced to endure one a year without being plagued by threats to survive yet another if we misbehave?"

Penelope's lips sank into a melodramatic frown. "There, there, Uncle. I will not permit the tyrant to force you to attend a second ball."

A tut alerted her to the presence of the tyrant in question—her Aunt Josephine. Ever the faithful co-conspirator, Penelope nudged her uncle and lifted a hand to her brow to sign the letter J, the agreed-upon name sign for her aunt.

He adjusted his posture to a slump and dishevelled his hair further. His niece did not take pleasure in his antics, or at least, she would never admit to it.

Upon rounding the corner, they discovered Lady Josephine Sedgewick—head of nearly every league in the county, founder of several more, sought-after conversationalist, enthralling orator, and, best of all, expert markswoman. Her posture was precise, her dress was perfect, and the barely bridled fire in her eyes was terrifying.

However, it was not her person that drew a toothy grin across Uncle Archie's face (after all, he saw his sister every day). No, it was the presence of two dragons snuggled up beside her on the bench.

The teacup-sized reptile of the pair, a female with coral feathers trimmed with gold and a frill that resembled a lady's collar, bounded over to Uncle Archie. With all the care of a papa, he scooped her into his arms, nuzzled her, and slipped her a treat.

A second, with fur and scales in a colour reminiscent of seashore sands, cocked his head to one side before looking to Aunt Josephine for approval. A barely perceptible nod sufficed. He bounced, literally, his wings aflutter, to Penelope, knowing she could be relied upon to fill her reticule with dried berries coated in sugar.

She had often marvelled at the contrariness of her family's tastes. Cerberus, her uncle's fanciful scaly companion named after Hades's three-headed dog, avoided muck and rain like the plague. Quite the opposite of her owner, who found a turn about the garden in a thunderstorm restorative.

Ambrose, her aunt's spunky dragon, revelled in rolling in a pile of leaves and often dug in the garden. His owner, on the other hand, never permitted one of her dark hairs to fall out of place. And while his scales were often smudged with mud, her fine black (yes, black, always black) gowns were impervious to puddles and dirt.

Though their appearances did not align, their personalities did—Cerberus was as squashy as a velvet cushion, and Ambrose as spirited as a dozen eight-year-olds.

"You two were complaining, I take it."

Her aunt's ability to guess the contents of conversations correctly had long stumped her niece. Penelope suspected that either she hid a touch of the seer within or (more likely) applied her deductive reasoning masterfully.

Uncle Archibald plopped next to his sister in as an ungentlemanlike a manner as possible. "No, we were commiserating."

Familiar with her brother's juvenile attempts to get her goat, she ignored him and fixed her hawk-like crystal blue eyes on her niece. "*You* look lovely this fine afternoon. What does the rest of your day hold?"

Penelope could have replied, "I intend to pose as my assistant's assistant to investigate a matter of import for a near neighbour." However, as she had yet to divulge her discreet investigations or her gifts, even to her uncle, she instead answered, "I intend to observe the decay of a skeleton I discovered in the forest. It has been an object of interest of mine for some time now."

"Anybody we know?" The wistful glint in her uncle's eye did not escape her notice.

"Unfortunately, no."

A stick that Ambrose had deposited at her feet claimed her attention. Although the miniature zilant lacked hind legs and had suffered a torn wing, he still managed to bounce high enough to look her directly in the eye and say, *Come now, throw the stick before I do something drastic and nibble on your shoe.*

{Narrator's Note: Ambrose was a zilant dragon. Like other zilants, he lacked hind legs. Unlike others of his kind, he was unable to fly due to a prior injury. Needless to say, the trapper responsible retired after a tête-à-tête with Josephine Sedgewick. And, no, it was not his head residing in a jar in the library. Well, probably not.}

She obliged, winning a nod of approval from her aunt. "Sounds like a delightful afternoon. Do be careful, though, dear. The number of predators afoot in the forest is astounding."

A familiar lump formed just under Penelope's twelfth rib. Indigestion or a heart attack, certainly not anything as fearsome as shame or one of those other complex emotions she tried not to dwell on.

Intent on proving herself trustworthy (unlike her uncle, who had intentionally loosened his cravat), she squared her shoulders to her aunt. "For the midges, I shall take a satchel of citronella and peppermint."

"Add basil for good measure. One can never be too careful." Her aunt angled her torso away from her brother, intent on ignoring him.

"Noted. And I shall take a pistol for . . ." *suspects, men with bad breath, and flirts* " . . . politicians; however, as they are busy spending their ill-gotten gains at the card tables, I feel quite certain I shall not have a cause to draw—"

"Have you quite finished?"

It was not Penelope her aunt addressed. As a last resort, her brother had undone the buttons at his wrists and begun to roll up his shirt cuffs. The horror! Gentlewomen should not be subjected to the sight of an Englishman's untanned forearms.

Uncle Archie smirked—delighted.

Aunt Josephine rolled her eyes—seriously displeased.

And Penelope turned her step towards the forest, a wry grin tugging at the corners of her lips.

As a child, she had learned three things about her aunt and uncle: one, they loved one another fiercely. Two, they each derived pleasure from goading the other—she with her precise manners and he with his lack thereof. And, finally, three, when they got into a tizzy, it was best to depart, as she lacked the self-control necessary to refrain from laughing.

# CHAPTER 5

## The Chapter with the Corpse

"On the matter of sugar, only Americans and criminals add it to their cup before the tea has been poured."

*Teatime: A Guide to Everyday Civility, page 78*

As the hired horse-drawn carriage emerged from the wood, its passengers were afforded a view of the Abbey, Sir Henry Pilkington's ancestral home. The carpenters who had breathed life into the looming stone structure had no doubt intended it to become the haunt of the souls who would meet their demise within its walls; however, unlike nearly every other manor in the county, not a single man, woman, or child had perished by poison, stabbing, or gunfire—quite disappointing, really.

"Do I look like a lady?"

Walt did *look* like a lady—a proper gentlewoman— the daughter of a country knight, perhaps. Black ringlets styled. Gloves on. Ribbons tied. Boots polished. Nothing to complain of, per se. However . . .

"A lady's breath does not usually smell of pipe tobacco and . . ." Penelope sniffed the air. "Is that brandy?"

"Just a sip." Walt accepted a peppermint-laced lozenge. "You and that nose! Always in my affairs."

"Since my nose keeps you in pipe tobacco and muslin, probably best not to criticise it." She smirked. "Besides, I do not criticise you for enjoying a drink, but rather, for not offering me a glass."

The pair shared a suppressed grin, the type known to those whose friendship is not founded on convention or obligation, but upon mutual respect and admiration.

Each lady had assumed their prescribed facade: Walt had transformed into Miss Patience Jones, the sleuth, with her flawless sandy skin and curled raven locks, while Penelope, with her sprite-like figure and false eyebrows, had shrunk into her role of Miss Prudence, the secretary. They wore coordinating empire-waisted gowns made of an airy fabric with faint flower-chain stripes intended to convey respectability.

Neither spoke as the rickety wheels clattered over the paving stones near the door. While Penelope mentally replayed her dealings with the family, her companion . . . Well, in all honesty, she might have dozed.

A quick exchange of a coin with the hired coachman, and Walt rapped at the door. Penelope noted the tip, tap of the footman's shoes in the hall—not the least bit hurried. The matter, then, had not filtered down to the staff. When he opened the door, his neutral expression confirmed as much.

They were led to the parlour. Thankfully, the footman did not enter the bookshelf-lined room, assuring the pair that their hostess would be with them shortly. Had he entered it or even given it a cursory glance, he would have ruined Penelope's day.

There, partially obscured by a pair of chairs, lay the maid—dead.

When Walt's keen eye noticed the girl slumped against the hearth, she let out a groan. "Oh, bother."

A squeal did not escape Penelope. Nor did her heart flutter with anticipation: her tummy rumbled from hunger, that was all. After all, death was a grave affair. {Reader, please do forgive my shameless pun.} However, as a scientist, she could not deny the good fortune that had befallen her. To discover a body before meddlesome men had sullied the scene was a treat.

Her assistant steered away from the fireplace and planted herself on the corner of the desk. "Is she dead?"

Before she squatted beside the body, Penelope laid her reticule underneath a chair. "Quite."

Before taking a mental inventory of the scene—no detail was insignificant—she took a breath to steady her hands.

*Penelope, we are professionals. We are equal to the task. Let us pull ourselves together and stop thinking in the first person plural.*

Her thoughts returned to the present—namely, the corpse.

Nineteen, maybe twenty, she would hazard. Dark freckles in April told her that the girl frequently walked out of doors without her bonnet. Though she took care with her appearance, as evidenced by her tidy ginger hair and a hint of rouge on the cheeks, her shoes were well-worn and had been repaired two . . . no, three times.

Her hands were dry from scrubbing floors. She must have been—

"Clearing the morning tea, I'd say."

Penelope pursed her lips. Interruptions, even of her inner dialogue, were not to be borne.

"Possibly." With care, she lifted her foot, examining the stockings, which were finer than she would have expected a maid could afford. "Rigor mortis has spread to her extremities. Uncle Archie and I deduced the process takes six to eight hours."

"Is that what you do in that fine house of yours? Study dead bodies?"

She ignored the fact that Walt had slipped a chocolate into her pocket. "Among other things, yes."

"If that is how the wealthy spend their evenings, no thanks; poverty is fine by me."

Walt understood the arch of her employer's eyebrow to mean, *Make yourself useful and riffle through the letters, if you please,* which she did.

Before surveying the body further, Penelope scanned the room. With the exception of a tray and accompanying tea service lying on the floor, it appeared in order. It was a standard English parlour—complete with squashy chairs, dark wooden bookshelves, a fireplace with a carved mantel, and a desk with spindly legs. Cosy, or it would have been if not for the corpse.

Which had nothing sinister to disclose. A pity. A wound at the back of the head had bled, staining the maid's crisp, white collar. "A trauma to the head was the cause."

Her assistant drew near, bending over the body, hands stuffed in her pockets. "A fall?"

34

"Perhaps. There are no defensive wounds to suggest a struggle." And there were not—not a scratch or bruise, neither on her wrists nor her throat. Penelope was tempted to classify it as an accident, and yet, a nagging sensation prodded her not to jump to conclusions.

*Steady*, she urged.

"Nor is the room in a state, except the tea things, of course."

"Rooms can be tidied, but . . ." With care, Penelope lifted a book or two and then a vase. As she suspected: dust—even the finest manors had it. Tempted as she was to straighten the spines and arrange them in alphabetical order, she did not. After all, a household ought to be permitted to organise its shelves as it saw fit, even if it was wrong.

"You are correct; the room does not indicate that she fought an attacker." Penelope gathered her skirts as she knelt beside the body once more. "Nor is her uniform rumpled. It's very neat— recently purchased, I'd wager."

"Except for the massive tea and milk stains across the front." Walt gestured to the plain teapot, teacup, saucer, plate, creamer, and silver spoon cast across the rug. Her eye lingered on the teaspoon, solid silver.

"Obviously." Her gaze flickered from Walt to the teaspoon, then back again. "Speaking of the tea, what do you observe?"

Walt tore her eyes away from the spoon. "It's been spilt."

Penelope blinked several times, which her assistant understood to mean, *You cannot be serious.*

With her hands on her hips, she dropped her gentlewoman accent. "There is only one cup and saucer, in't there?"

"Clearly." Penelope lifted it. With care, she swiped her little finger across the brown residue dried on the side of the cup—tea without sugar or milk. She pressed her hand against the stained rug and the maid's uniform. Both were nearly dry.

Turning her back to her assistant, she cradled the cup in her hands and listened. A sensation of being submerged in scalding water flashed through her body. As the cup fell to the carpet, two or three rude words slipped through her gritted teeth.

She should have expected that. Eavesdropping on the histories of knives, guns, and cookware was never pleasant—a novice mistake.

Out of the corner of her eye, she caught Walt secreting a third chocolate in her pocket. Having been spotted, Walt froze, resembling a child sneaking biscuits.

Penelope folded her arms.

Walt pursed her lips. "Listen, you! Who will notice? Besides, if they do, I wager they'll blame it on the maid. And, well, what will they do? Fire her?"

To the surprise of the chocolate thief, Penelope held out her hand. "It is impolite not to share."

Had they not been intent on avoiding discovery, the pair would have burst into laughter raucous enough to awaken even the maid.

Instead, Penelope popped the chocolate into her mouth and continued. "As for the tea, it would appear as though more than one cup remained in the pot."

"Scandalous." And it was. Much like an opportunity to make a sarcastic quip, tea ought never to be wasted.

"Indeed."

Whilst Penelope finished making a mental sketch of the placement of the body, Walt destroyed the evidence of her misdeeds by stuffing the chocolates into her mouth (without dribbling on the rug, mind you), after which she patted her lips with her handkerchief. "Have you seen enough?"

Penelope straightened her glasses, ensuring that the charm disguising her appearance was in order. "Quite. I shall alert the staff."

Walt leaned over the maid, near, but not too near. "And I shall appear to be inspecting the body."

"Do you think I should faint?"

"Nah, best not overdo it."

With that, Penelope flung open the door to the hall.

# CHAPTER 6

## The Chapter with the Tryst

"Remember how tender a thing a woman's
reputation is, how hard to preserve and when lost
how impossible to recover."

*Fordyce's Sermons to Young Ladies*

After the ladies had been shuffled out of the parlour,
Lady Pilkington, in an uncommon display of good sense,
ordered tea and cakes to be served in the drawing room.
After all, nothing soothes the nerves like well-brewed
leaves and sugar.

"Please accept my apologies." Once she had claimed
the seat opposite Walt and Penelope, she preened,
smoothing her gauzy muslin skirts and fiddling with the
bracelet of iridescent scales no larger than droplets. At
barely forty, Lady Pilkington, with her honey-blonde hair
and doe-eyes, was still considered handsome and, through
the application of a judicious quantity of creams and
salves, intended to remain so for quite some time. "An
unfortunate accident, or so I have been told."

"Do not distress yourself on our behalf." Walt shook her head with the delicacy of a duchess. Had they not been in the presence of a client, Penelope would have congratulated her on her adroit performance. "May I enquire as to the young maid's name?"

"Grace . . ."

The creak of the drawing-room door announced the arrival of the tea and cakes. As servants were renowned gossips, the ladies naturally paused their conversation, giving Penelope a moment to admire the room.

As Aunt Josephine found the Pilkingtons to be "vainglorious twits with the brains and morals of a brickbat" (and that was putting it gently), Penelope had not endured their hospitality often. Therefore, she took an interest in the layout of the drawing room. She surveyed it for signs of hidden stairwells or security wards—none. How unoriginal. The room was fashionable without being ostentatious, decorated in rich goldenrods and pale pinks. Lovely, had it not been so unremarkable.

Cups of the dark, bitter liquid were served. This tea set was not part of that which lay on the parlour floor. Serving refreshments on the other would have been a bit macabre, she supposed.

As the secretary, Penelope was not expected to converse with the hostess, nor think, for that matter, which served her purposes well. Freed from the shackles of civility, she could observe undisturbed.

For instance, Walt's lingering glance at the spoon resting on her saucer did not escape her notice. To pass the time, she determined that it would "disappear" from her saucer in six to ten minutes.

The footman, an eye-catching fellow who walked with a swagger, exited at last. No sooner had the door clicked shut than Lady Pilkington resumed their discourse. "Grace Stewart. That is the girl's name. Or is it Sullivan? It hardly matters. I have entrusted the arrangements to my butler. He will see that her family is notified."

"Then she has family nearby?" Walt patted her pinched lips with a lace handkerchief. The tendons in her jaw and throat were taut, indicating that she, too, found the Pilkingtons' manners lacking. Impressed by her assistant's patience, Penelope considered sending her a tin of pipe tobacco later on as a token of her appreciation.

"An uncle, I believe. Or brother? Pity." Lady Pilkington sipped her tea, unconcerned. One would have thought they were discussing the weather rather than the untimely passing of a young girl.

{Narrator's Note: The reader will be distressed to learn that after the events of this novel, Sir Henry Pilkington received a questionable tip regarding the prices of coal. He invested a large sum. Unfortunately, the family was forced to let their home and settle in Bath. Pity.}

Setting aside her cup on a table no wider than a dinner plate, Lady Pilkington began, "No doubt you are curious as to why I asked you here today."

The pair nodded.

"Are you at all familiar with my daughter, Miss Pilkington?"

Walt folded her hands in her lap. "We have never met, but I know of her. She is . . ." Her employer, seated to the lady's left, just out of view, signed the number she sought. ". . . one and twenty, correct? And your . . ."

*Only,* she signalled.

". . . only child."

"Yes." Lady Pilkington nibbled on a vanilla sponge fairy cake with buttered icing, careful not to dislodge crumbs that would sully her dress. (At least *she* had good table manners.) "Rose is . . ."

*Naive. Silly. Vapid. Think of a nice word* . . . Penelope bit into a seed cake. Dry. *Does "not a bore" count? Or a boar, actually.*

A scene of the young Miss Pilkington staring like an Irish elk with its antlers lodged in the branches of an apple tree rose in her mind. Aunt Josephine had made a witty remark during a visit, which had earned her the laughter and smiles of her guests, all except Miss Pilkington, who had instead stared, confused. Dear girl, so lovely yet so . . . well . . . best leave it there.

". . . and innocent girl—wholly unspoilt."

{Oh yes, her mama was speaking. Reader, do forgive me. That was horribly impolite of me, to insert an entire scene in the middle of her discourse. I do apologise.

I have done it again, haven't I? Where were we? Oh, yes.}

Lady Pilkington rose and crossed to the mantel. Her fine blush gown draped over her curves. She pretended to adjust the position of several trinkets, but in actuality, she observed herself in the gilded mirror. "Are you familiar with Mr Montagu, heir to the Lord Viscount Montagu's estate?"

Walt said she had after Penelope dipped her chin.

"Of late, Mr Montagu and my daughter have formed an attachment."

Word of their attachment had spread far and wide throughout the county. Although the Pilkingtons were flush with capital, Sir Lawrence was merely a knight. Mr Tobias Montagu lacked for nothing; at least, he would not once the current viscount passed. He was to inherit a title and a substantial estate, and he had pleasing manners and a nice set of teeth. Though not local, he visited his uncle and aunt often enough to have earned a reputation as a pleasant sort of gentleman.

"Her father and I had believed he would declare his intentions before the ball next week, yet . . ." She withdrew a letter from a locked box on the mantel. She crossed the room, resumed her seat, and handed the missive to Walt.

"This morning, I discovered this letter. It had been slipped under my door in the night."

Walt read the letter, careful not to betray her interest or lack thereof. It took all of Penelope's will not to snatch it from her hands; instead, she waited patiently (sort of) for her turn to peruse its contents.

*Dearest Mama,*
*By the time you are in receipt of this letter, I shall*
*be far away. While I know it was your hope that I*
*wed Mr M, I cannot. My heart belongs to another,*

*a captain whom I met in Cardiff last year.*
*Please forgive me, Mama. When we present ourselves*
*as husband and wife, I hope you will receive us.*
*Yours,*
*Rose*

Had she been alone, she would have permitted herself to use her gift to listen to the letter and discern its history. However, as the tell-tale signs of a psychometrist at work were difficult to miss (vacant expression, dribbling, etc.), she contended herself with the briefest of tastes, sensing anxiety and foreboding. Begrudgingly, she returned the letter to its owner.

On cue, Walt asked, "Are you at all acquainted with this captain?"

As Penelope had hazarded she would, the lady crossed to the fire and tossed the letter onto the logs. The girl's dear mama would naturally wish to erase every trace of her daughter's foolish misstep. "Not to my knowledge."

"And had you noted an alteration in her behaviour prior?"

"No, none." The three women were entranced by the blackened paper recoiling at the touch of the flame, curling in on itself.

In a voice no louder than the sizzle of the fire dancing on the hearth, Lady Pilkington cursed. "Foolish girl."

Walt stole a glance at her employer. A shake of the head was her sole reply. No, Lady Pilkington was not one to seek solace from strangers. While other clients would permit a frown or a kind word as a token of support, this client would not.

Penelope sipped her tea. Walt smoothed her skirt. The moment faded, then vanished.

After an uncomfortable exchange, nothing resets the tone quite like a subtle clearing of the throat, which Walt executed splendidly. "While I do sympathise with your predicament, I am not certain how I can be of service."

Shaken from her abstraction, Lady Pilkington turned. "At present, no one knows of her elopement. We have arranged matters so that our acquaintances will believe she has gone to visit a cousin who was recently delivered of her first child."

While Penelope did not like this woman, she had to admire her cunning. Her plan bought her time to recover her daughter, potentially averting a scandal.

"I would like you to find her. If she is married, so be it, but if she is not . . ."

Walt spoke the words they all were thinking. "Return her to your care discreetly?"

"Precisely. If you discover her unwed, you will bring her to this address." From the pages of a leather-bound book resting on a table, she withdrew a folded paper, thick, likely containing notes.

Penelope had to admire Walt's self-possession. Usually, when she received a letter, she tore it open with the fervour of a dragon discovering a chest of gold or a bowl of treats. Instead, she slid it into her reticule.

{Narrator's Note: While it is widely known that dragons are naturally drawn to precious stones and metals, what has only recently been discovered is their near-equal adoration for sweets.}

"We are to host a ball on Monday, so time is of the essence." Lady Pilkington rose briskly, signalling that their interview had drawn to a close. "Will there be anything further?"

Without a glance at her employer, Walt placed her teacup and saucer, sans spoon, on the tea tray. "No, that should be sufficient."

Penelope had been incorrect; Walt had absconded with the spoon in under five minutes, a record.

# CHAPTER 7

## The Chapter with the Sneeze

"Fortunate are those who possess the gift of
psychometry. To envision whispers from an item's
history has several practical applications."

*A Case for the Legalisation of the Practice of Magic by*
*Benjamin Franklin*

Whenever Penelope searched a client's bedchamber, she
hoped to discover they had a dark side lurking beneath the
layers of muslin and lace, or the least, an interesting side.

Alas, few ladies and even fewer gentlemen did. Most
were wholly unimaginative in their vices, sticking with the
obvious ones like gambling, charm addictions, and secret
love nests. Just once, she longed to discover that a neighbour posed as a Grecian model for sculptors (yes, *that* sort)
or kept a sanctuary for woolly rhinos in the north country.

Unsurprisingly, dear Rose did neither. Even the diaries were wholly unimaginative. They contained pages
upon pages of Hunt sightings, midnight trysts (which did
not even deserve the honour of being called a "tryst", as

nothing more than "longing glances" had been exchanged. How unoriginal!), and several mentions of the yeti.

{Narrator's Note: Yetis are known by a host of names throughout the world—Sasquatch, Bigfoot, Yowie, Grey Man, and Dzu-teh. In Alderwood, the recent arrival of a yeti had caused quite a stir. In fact, there were no fewer than three clubs dedicated to spotting him. Half of their meetings were spent discussing how they should feel to meet the man himself, and one-third were dedicated to arguing, leaving little time to seek the man himself.}

Given that half of her entries had undoubtedly been exaggerated, Penelope was flabbergasted that Miss Pilkington had been bold enough to risk an adventure as improper as an elopement. The captain in question must have been quite persuasive.

After Penelope had sent Walt packing, she had been left in peace to peruse the contents of Rose's desk and the novels tucked under her mattress. The novels, too tame to have necessitated hiding, did not contain pressed flowers or scraps of paper bearing a man's name. The drawers stuffed with her stockings and underclothes had barely been touched, indicating she had packed in haste.

Alone, Penelope took care to listen to the dresses, quills, and ribbons, hoping to catch a glimpse of the young man. All they shared were fleeting glimpses of the girl's daily life—walks through the forest, tea time, and church on Sundays.

This was unsurprising. Like people, objects do not retain every memory. In her experience, only powerful ones left an impression.

Once she had pried up every loose floorboard and searched a secret passageway accessed by pressing a plaster flower near the fireplace, she slipped downstairs. If the reader remembers, Penelope had "conveniently" left her reticule under the chair in the parlour. This was not an original ploy, of course, but useful. It permitted her to return to a scene, providing a ready excuse should she be discovered (which she never was, but still).

The parlour had been tidied, and by tidied I mean that Grace's body had been removed, though the tea stains remained on the Persian rug. Although the death of the girl was not her case to solve per se, she was curious: could she discover the murderer (if one even existed)?

Without a corpse cluttering the room, she was free to reenact the scene. Penelope stood at the desk, imaginary tray in hand, and stepped backwards. The heel of her boot caught on the rug. It was not implausible that the maid had tripped.

"Please, ma'am, can Susan not clean the parlour today?" Though the oak door muffled the voices, it was apparent that the speaker was a young woman.

*Oh, bother. Maids.* While an amateur sleuth might have dropped to the floor and rolled underneath the chaise longue, Penelope never rolled, nor was she an amateur. She did not dart across the room pell-mell either. Instead, she weaved through the high-backed chairs and around the desk to the window, where she secreted herself behind the heavy damask curtains.

"You will clean it if you want to keep your position." The second voice was that of the middle-aged housekeeper: Mrs Bates.

The latch clicked, and the door slid open. Two sets of shoes tip-tapped across the floor.

"But, ma'am, my aunt said that spirits linger for two days after death. And if you disturb them, they will haunt you for the rest of your life." Penelope's ear, rather than her eye, told her the maid had remained in the hall. A third person must have entered, then.

"Balderdash!" Penelope could imagine the prim housekeeper tapping her foot impatiently and checking her watch. "What is the world coming to? Girls believing that spirits have nothing better to do than linger in the parlour."

In the girls' defence, once the House of Lords had decreed that the Folk and magic, in fact, exist, one could not ignore the possibility of visitors from the beyond.

In a terse tone, the housekeeper insisted, "Get in here and dust the mantel, or find yourself a new position."

"Yes, ma'am." The voice of a second maid agreed with the first.

The shifting of books and vases was interrupted only by the rustles of the maids' skirts. Penelope leaned against the glass, warmed by the rays of the afternoon sun that had peeked out from behind the clouds. The heat pressed through her clothes, reminding her of a basket of laundered linens recently removed from the clothesline. Had she not been crammed behind a curtain, scarcely able to breathe, she would have enjoyed the opportunity to rest.

A gasp ruined her respite.

"I just felt her spirit pass through me!"

The second girl took no pains to disguise an exasperated sigh. "Nonsense. Do you really believe in spirits and spectres?" Her voice was sharp, with a frayed quality, as though she had just recovered from a cold (or had stayed awake until two in the morning drinking, but you did not hear that from me).

"Do you not?"

"No," she answered curtly. "Dusting the parlour and library always makes my nose itch. I only said those things to shirk it off if I could."

A scrubbing sound accompanied by the sloshing of water indicated that one of the girls was cleaning the stains from the rug. "They are saying it was an accident; I think she could have been killed by a jealous lover."

The second maid scoffed. "Murdered? Lord, who'd want to murder dull old Grace? Jealous lover, my aunt Fanny."

"She could have one!" The pitch of the girl's voice could have shattered glass. Clearly, she did not like being dismissed. "Just last week, the footman—"

"Frank the footman? Oh, he is a dish."

Penelope, much to her chagrin, found a dopey smile had sneaked onto her face at the mention of the Greek god masquerading as a footman. Though his vacant expression counteracted any visceral attraction she felt, she could not disagree with the maid; he was devastatingly handsome.

"No, it was Jim, but I'll get to Frank in a moment. He told her she was the 'prettiest girl in the village,' and you'll never guess how she replied."

"How?"

*Yes, how?*

"She slapped him."

"No!"

*No!*

The rustle of rags and the splashing of water ceased. This was, after all, delicious gossip, and one should always devote one's entire attention in such situations.

"Yes!" The younger maid's voice was almost a shout. "Slapped him so hard his cheek was red for half of the morning. She told him to never take such a familiar tone with her again. Then, later that day, Frank punched him. Makes one wonder if the two aren't connected. Doesn't it?"

*Indeed, it does,* Penelope agreed.

After a few moments, the scrape of the brush against the fibres of the rug continued. "Still, just because a girl rebuffs a man's attentions doesn't mean Frank, or anyone else for that matter, was her lover."

"Or perhaps she'd overheard something she shouldn't have?" wondered the first maid.

The girl had a valid point.

"Keep that nose in the bucket and out of other people's affairs. She had a fall. Bad luck, that's all."

The clattering of the metal pail drowned out the younger girl's response. Penelope leaned forward a fraction of an inch, careful not to disturb the window dressings. All she caught were the words "debts," "Philadelphia" (or Pilkington. She could not be certain which the girl actually said), and "secret."

"Are you certain?!" Whatever Penelope had missed had been interesting enough to shake the disinterest from the second girl's voice. Drat! "He always seemed like such a respectable—ACHOOO!"

Penelope gave a start, disrupting the rose-coloured curtains. Her body froze while her mind reeled with curses. She had never been caught snooping, and she was not about to tarnish her track record because of dust up a silly girl's nose. Breathlessly, she waited.

"As I was saying, if you want to keep your job, you'll keep your theories to yourself. They pay us to clean, not ask questions."

Penelope rested her head against the window as the tension drained from her body.

The maids continued their work in silence, shifting the odd paper or trinket. By the time they collected their supplies and the door had been shut, Penelope felt stiff from leaning unnaturally against the window pane for half an hour.

Before she emerged into the hall, she considered what she had heard. The gossip was curious . . . yet it was not her concern.

As she headed into the hall and out of the front door, Penelope made a decision: she would put this nonsense out of her mind. She had been hired to discover an eloped girl, not investigate a murder an accident. With that, she filed the incident away, determined not to devote another moment to it.

# CHAPTER 8

## The Chapter with the Revolutionary Understanding of Genetics

"The benevolent hand of nature bestows 'the gift' upon women twice as frequently as she does upon men, demonstrating her boundless wisdom."

*Mary Wollstonecraft*

When Penelope entered the library the next morning, Uncle Archie had already piled his plate high with honey cakes and golden brioche bread. The yeasty fragrance of fresh-baked breads and pastries made her heady with a feeling of home.

A grin was greeting enough for his niece. His hair, once dark like hers but now streaked with silver, stood on end. Evidence of his valet's attempts to tame his appearance was obvious in his ironed shirt, which would undoubtedly wrinkle of its own volition within the hour. His eyes roved the pages of a scientific paper with glee.

From the sideboard, she selected fresh blueberries, foraged by her aunt on her daily walk, and a honey cake with a spoonful of blackthorn preserve. Since her uncle's dragon occupied the chair adjacent to her owner, she selected the one opposite him.

Cerberus peeked at her from beneath her wings, the colours of stained glass, before covering her eyes once more. This was not a snub; the teacup faedragon was infamous for sleeping until noon.

A spread of books, rumpled academic papers, and notes served as a tablecloth. Among the titles were *The Folk: Fact or Fantasy*, *The Science of Heredity*, and *Magic: Spirit or Science*. They had spilt onto the rug, a waterfall of parchment and ink. As this room rarely welcomed guests, it had been transformed into a haven for the family—a place for their eccentricities to roam.

A hundred years ago, the library had been expanded to double its size. Floor-to-ceiling shelves encased in carved mahogany housed thousands of volumes. In her youth, their multicoloured spines had fascinated her. On any given day, she could be found stretched across a rug, memorizing lineages or diagrams of ships. This place had been, to her, a wonderland, permitting her to escape the confines of her station. It had lent wings to her ideas until the day she had courage enough to begin her own albeit secret enterprise.

Loose scraps of paper, potted plants of exotic varieties, and models of flying machines were tucked between the volumes, a testament to her uncle's varying interests. Opposite the white marble fireplace spanned an arched window that opened to a view of the grounds. In front of the window, the family had placed a table for breakfast or midday tea.

After satisfying her stomach's rumbling with a few bites of bread, Penelope picked up one of the volumes. "I see that you and Lord Alderwood have selected a fresh topic to . . ." *bicker about* ". . . debate."

{Narrator's Note: The Lord Alderwood is indeed *that* Lord Alderwood—earl, theoretical mathematician, culinary genius, and botanist. For the purposes of our story, he is also Uncle Archie's dearest friend, so long as they do not inhabit the same room. In that case, calling them archnemesis would be putting it mildly.}

The advantage of communicating in sign language rather than spoken English was that one could talk with one's mouth full. The disadvantage lay in the risk that you might topple a teapot amidst an impassioned conversation or fling crumbs across the table.

Hence, it was not impolite for her uncle to rip off a piece of brioche and stuff it in his mouth before responding. "Yes, our topic of study this month is the Folk."

Had Uncle Archie not been preoccupied with topping up his teacup, he might have noticed her shift in her seat— evidence that his niece had a secret other than the fact that she privately investigated delicate matters for ladies. She also possessed a gift—two, in fact. But, of course, Reader, you knew as much.

Her ability to detect magical items had emerged early on. Since her youngest years, her nose would itch interminably. At first, her parents had believed she suffered from hay fever, so they approached a herbalist for sundry cures (which never helped in the least). It was when they visited one such shop that she discovered the true source of her ailment.

While her mama browsed the shelves, a young Penelope tried on a beauty talisman, giggling when it made her eyes appear unusually round. Not two snaps later, she began to sneeze. Her mother, assuming the odours of the herbs and salves had triggered the fit, removed the charm, intending to lead her outside. But as soon as the charm had been set aside, her symptoms ceased. It was on that day that Penelope and her mother understood she had the gift of detection, or sniffing as it was known colloquially, permitting her to sense the presence of charms, talismans, and magical creatures.

Her second gift emerged in the latter years of her childhood. It first showed itself when she wore her mother's locket for the first time after her death. One moment, she was admiring the lock of her mother's hair it contained. The next, she was transported to the day her mama had received the necklace, her sixteenth birthday.

Over time, she would learn to summon her ability to listen. Yet, even before she had, she had learned not to divulge such secrets, not even to her aunt or uncle. After all, she had been born into a time when magic had not yet been legalized, let alone accepted, and even when it had, its practice was not condoned among the upper crust.

Penelope poured herself a cup of tangy Earl Grey, careful to add a spoonful of honey and stir it well. "A worthy endeavour, Uncle. And what is your hypothesis?"

"The Earl hypothesises that the source of the Folk's abilities is not spiritual, but biological, sprouting from their heredity, not the beyond."

"Do you agree?"

"Yes. Surprisingly, I do." His hazel eyes, framed by wiry eyebrows, twinkled with delight. "It is perfectly sound to conclude that a person's ability to find lost objects or cure minor illnesses is inherited, much like ginger hair or blue eyes."

He paused to butter his bread. After savouring a bite, he continued. "Similarly, a parent may pass to their child natural athleticism or artistic talent."

Cerberus lifted her head, earning a tender scratch near her chin. Uncle Archie received a nip on the fingers as thanks before she tucked her nose under her wing once more. "Indeed, while there are those who achieve greatness, others are born with an innate proclivity for arts, sciences, etc."

To say that Penelope was unsurprised would be an understatement. If you were to gather one hundred Folk into a room, slip them a truth tincture, and ask whether their gifts were of nature or of the divine, ninety-six would respond, "Of nature. All the hand-waving, eye-rolling, and chanting is for show. If customers knew all it took to treat a strained thumb was for me to touch it, I could never persuade them to buy my salves or tinctures." Or something like that. As for the other four Folk, well, there are always outliers.

She did, however, disagree with her uncle on one point: not all Folk sprang from magical lineages. "What, then, of those whose family has never had a gift?"

One would have thought she had asked him whether he would like a box of sweets. A fire kindled within his eyes, lighting his expression ablaze. His signs became exaggerated, filling the space around his body. "I have long theorised that our cells contain within them a set of instructions which science has yet to discover."

His niece wisely moved the teapot to the sideboard.

"At conception, the instructions from the mother combine with those of the father. The ensuing child, then, is a combination of his or her parents' instructions."

"Logically." Her encouraging grin spurred him on.

"Perhaps, in cases where neither parent has a gift, a line may have been copied incorrectly. Much like myself and my quirks." He paused, drawing his hands closer to his body.

One can be proud yet still struggle to accept oneself precisely as they are. As a child, Penelope delighted in her uncle's eccentricities, yet as an adult, she wondered whether they were a sort of distraction intended to keep the world at arm's length. Her heart ached at the notion that his title of Sir Loon had been a shield, not a medal.

She reached across the table and squeezed his hand. "In my eyes, Uncle, you are profoundly perfect. I would not alter you in the least."

They held one another's gaze for a moment, soaking in the warmth of the other's expression. She memorised each line, each fleck of gold in his eyes, and the tears in his eyes suggested that he thanked whatever deity had set the galaxies spinning for the honour of calling her his niece.

Penelope returned the teapot to the table. "Do you intend to meet in person?"

"What a ghastly idea!" Her uncle's lip curled. "In person! Why would I do such a silly thing? No, no. I barely tolerate him in letters. It would mean the ruination of our partnership if we ever socialised."

The sound of her aunt's voice in the hall drove her to her feet. Though she welcomed Aunt Josephine's company, she had several matters to attend to and could not spare another half an hour. After stroking Cerberus's back and planting a kiss on her uncle's rough cheek, she asked, "Have you the letter?"

Uncle Archie appeared nonchalant as he withdrew a blank envelope from his pocket, though his niece knew better. "Yes. Do see that it is delivered today."

For a decade, every Sunday, she had carried a letter to a locked box at the edge of their property. She knew not to whom the letters were written nor why he could not deliver them himself.

"Of course." With the letter stowed in her bag, she paused near the door. "Uncle, have you ever left a pot of tea barely touched?"

He started. "Lord, no. Who would ever do such a thing?"

With that, she turned the knob and slipped from the room. A feeling arose within her that made her insides feel as wobbly as a deer wearing ice-skates. She shoved it into the deepest recesses of her mind, burying it under facts about fungi.

The tidy walls of propriety and manners kept her safe, untouched by the less desirable effects of being a woman with brains and magic. Had she been honest with herself, she would have acknowledged that she, too, struggled to accept herself wholly; however, with a girl to find and a suspicious death to ignore, she had no time for such reflections.

# CHAPTER 9

## The Chapter with the Running (Ugh!)

"WARNING:
If you see a drake, run to the nearest tower.
If there is no tower nearby, climb a tree."

*A sign posted in the Forest of Dean, 1810*

The town of Alderwood did not merely border the Forest of Dean; it stood in the midst of it. While its ancient trees might have spilt onto every thoroughfare and estate, it was its moss that drew the town's ire. The good townspeople waged war against the dewy green invader. It grew in the most inconvenient places, coating everything that did not have a pulse (and a few things that did).

Though few townsfolk ventured far from town into the heart of the wood, none could escape passing through its borders. For safety's sake, paths had been marked, lined with limestone to reflect the light even on evenings when the moon shone dimly.

Paths that cut through the ancient groves led to the occasional platform, constructed not for entertainment but to escape rogue drakes, boars, or Irish elks. Wards to alert travellers to the presence of dragons were placed at intervals. However, they were not foolproof, as they had been known to clang when approached by a flock of swans. Given that tourism brought a steady stream of adventure seekers to Alderwood, such measures had become necessary to avoid bad press (and deaths, of course).

As to more fanciful creatures who were rumoured to dwell in the shadows, common sense alone could protect a traveller from such; however, as the country had a deficit of that commodity, many had ventured into the wood, never to return.

Penelope took one such path that morning. She was armed with prudence, a bag of treats (for any wild dragons or badgers), and a loaded pistol. After she delivered her uncle's letter, she intended to proceed to town, after which she would visit the slighted Mr Montagu's aunt. Aunts were excellent sources of information, prone to gossip, and often lacking in self-control.

Rather than take the crooked way that led into a maze of moss-enshrouded ravines, she selected a plainer path, hoping to avoid the tourists. She strolled the packed earth trails, revelling the calls of songbirds in the treetops overhead.

As she pushed deeper into the wood, wisps of mist still clung to the boughs of the bare deciduous trees. Buds had only just begun to appear. Soon, the forest would be transformed into a verdant fairyland once more.

When her path wound through a grove of pine, the vanilla fragrance of their sap danced on a breeze. She inhaled, marvelling as ancient yew and oak spread their arms protectively over their young saplings. Fern carpeted the forest floor, providing a home to all manner of creatures. It was truly magical, and if the characters of legends did, in fact, exist, then this place, protected against the tyranny of men, was where they would dwell.

For no reason she could pin down precisely, her hand slipped to her bonnet and drew out a blade disguised as a feather. Her other hand slid into the harness sewn into her spencer and withdrew a pistol no longer than the palm of her hand. A hush dripped from the dewy branches, spreading across the forest floor.

Silence. Even the wind dared not whisper. Penelope held her breath.

"Right this way! Careful of the roots, ladies. Wouldn't want to twist an ankle, would we?"

Blast! Tourists. Penelope broke into a sprint towards the disconnected voice.

"As it is daytime, we'll not . . ."

There, partially obscured by a boulder, stood the guide—a sallow man with no chin—and a party of three gentlemen and two ladies. Eyes wide, they fell speechless at the sight of a gentlewoman, skirts pulled above her knees, running.

She could have attempted to reason with them. She could have pleaded. However, as time was of the essence, she opted for the most logical course: lying.

"Over there, a wyrm! It is heading this way!"

As wyrms were known to fancy the taste of men's flesh, the three gentlemen, two ladies, and guide hastened after her.

The nearest tower lay to the south. She trusted the game trails to guide her. As she crested a hill, she heard it—the clanging of wards, triggered by the presence of magic. Her senses reached out. A darkness was closing upon them.

A woman shouted from the platform ahead. "It is a drake! Hurry!"

As a narrator, it is my job to build tension, to describe how our heroine experienced an existential crisis. For instance, she could swear that, if she lived, she would reconnect with an old flame or beg forgiveness of a friend she had once betrayed.

A tourist could trip over a branch, twisting his ankle . . .

A heroic knight could arrive . . .

A forest dragon could swoop down from the treetops . . .

And while all of this would make for excellent storytelling, it would be a lie. Sorry to disappoint.

First Penelope, then the tourists, arrived at the rickety stairs unharmed, though winded and in need of a comb. They dashed up them, taking two at a time. Once she had reached the top, she crossed the platform to the bannister to stand beside a woman, the one who had shouted the warning. There below, not ten yards from the platform's support beams, were the drakes—a pack of three young males.

The lithe dragons, muscled and wingless, circled the platform. Their colouring shifted from a dark green to a pale yellow as they stepped into the sun. They were known as masters of camouflage, able to ambush dragonkind and humans alike.

Though attacks were rare, as forest dragons kept them at bay, they did happen. Had Penelope not sensed what scant magic they did possess (the little that remained when their lust for pain had consumed them), that day might have ended quite differently.

"Glad you survived. I do not know how I would have faced your aunt had I seen you devoured by a pack of drakes."

Penelope turned. Beside her stood the woman who had shouted the warning, a force of nature she fondly referred to as Mrs Abigail Stevenson, her aunt's dearest friend.

"It would have been better if you had fled the country." Penelope leaned over the railing to get a better look at them. After all, few people saw a drake and lived to tell the tale. Though they were compact, coming just to her chest, she could feel their power ripple outward.

"Impossible. I have a game of whist to beat your aunt at next Thursday," replied Mrs Stevenson. It may be impolite to describe a lady as voluptuous, yet no other epithet could so succinctly describe the woman who greeted her.

Penelope, whose thin frame had never been the object of lust, had long noticed men's thinly veiled attempts not to ogle Mrs Stevenson. Besides having been blessed with more curves than a mountain road, she had a Grecian nose, startling blue eyes, and lips that were almost indecent. Even at fifty-odd years old, she was striking.

Penelope ignored the stitch in her side. Her eyes drifted to the tourists at the other end of the platform. They leaned against the pine that shot straight through its middle, their chests heaving. It was then that she noticed it: they were one shy. "Have you spotted the guide?"

"The peaky one with the loud voice?" Mrs Stevenson had a defiant streak that one could not help but admire. Contrariness was a quality Penelope thought all ladies ought to endeavour to develop.

Penelope nodded.

"The {this word has been omitted as it may be deemed offensive} climbed the first tree he could scale." Mrs Stevenson glanced back at the tourists, who had barely begun to catch their breath. "Sadly, the pack let him be, though I wonder if they will circle back to catch him unawares?"

"One can only hope."

Common sense and widely distributed pamphlets instructed sanctuary seekers to remain aloft for at least half an hour (or until they heard the drakes' cries indicating that they had dined elsewhere). The two ladies made use of one of the benches that had been provided by the good townspeople, leaving the other two to the tourists. The bench upon which they were seated bore a plaque.

*In Memory of Gerald – 1720 to 1807*

"A little macabre, is it not?" Mrs Stevenson gestured to the plaque. "Did he perish nearby, having been hunted down by the drakes, or did he simply die of age? A little context would be helpful."

Penelope chuckled.

"Speaking of nothing in any way connected with this bench, I trust your aunt and uncle are well."

"Yes. I left Uncle Archibald in the throes of research."

The lady tipped her chin, a pleasant smile curving the corners of her lips.

"And Aunt Josephine had yet to make an appearance in the breakfast room. Are you on your way to visit her?"

"No, though I would prefer it if I were. This morning takes me to town. Perhaps this afternoon I shall stop by your aunt's house for tea."

*And gossip.* Penelope grinned. "What takes you to—"

"And the gentleman lost a hundred quid in one hand. Can you believe it?" One of the young men had taken on the role of storyteller. He stood, gesturing wildly.

The arch of Mrs Stevenson's brow communicated, *I wonder if it was one of our acquaintances?*

*Probable, as nearly half the town gambles, though only a tenth will admit to it,* conveyed the subtle shrug of Penelope's shoulders.

"There was this rumpled fellow, grey hair standing on end as though he'd been struck by lightning." The storyteller gestured wildly, knocking his own hat off to reveal a receding hairline. As quickly as he could, he replaced it and continued. "Said nothing the entire time, just watched . . ."

With a sidelong glance, Mrs Stevenson remarked, *I did not know your uncle was a gambler.*

*He is not,* bristled Penelope. She thrust her chin into the air. *He is developing a formula to predict the outcome of certain card games.*

"Then he made odd shapes with his hands like this." The foul creature began to wave his arms about while his friends laughed.

Penelope was on her feet in a blink, tugging at her dagger with her right hand. Unbridled fury transf-ormed her impish face into that of a vengeful spirit. The look of horror in his eye as she approached . . . Let us just say he had to launder his pants that afternoon.

Just as she was about to strike, another figure stepped between them, arm cocked to deliver a brilliant blow to his beak-like nose. The man crumpled to the floor, clutching his snout and cursing.

Mrs Stevenson shook her hand as she towered above the prostrate man. "You have just insulted one of the most brilliant minds of this century." She leaned close. "Never—Do—It—Again."

Penelope slipped her dagger into its sheath and spat on the man before turning to her friend. "To town?"

The ladies stepped past the dumbstruck man and descended the stairs, feeling more at ease among the creatures who called the forest home than the animals they had left in the tower.

The forest was alive once more with the song of birds and the chattering of squirrels. Penelope sensed a lightness in the air. The drakes had moved on, though the clouds had not. A dark sea blanketed the sky, threatening to tarnish the day with a downpour.

As they walked, the ladies chit-chatted about recent events until their conversation turned to a topic of interest.

Mrs Stevenson began, "Perhaps you have not yet heard, but a young maid suffered a tragic accident at the Abbey yesterday—a Grace . . ."

*Sullivan. Grace Sullivan.* Though Penelope wished to clap her hands and squeal like a schoolgirl, she remained calm, giving off a polite air of disinterested interest.

"Sullivan. I have been tasked by the Ladies' Aid Society with delivering a basket of foodstuffs to the grieving brother."

It took every ounce of control Penelope possessed to restrain her lips from curling into an eager expression. "Yes, I heard of the death. A shame, one so young."

Mrs Stevenson dipped her chin. Her long fingers picked a flower as they passed. She twirled it before tucking it behind her ear, lost in thought.

Penelope took a breath, careful not to appear *too* eager. "As I have no pressing matters to attend to, will you permit me to deliver the basket in your stead? I . . ." *Excuse. Think of an excuse.* "I have been remiss in my charity work of late and would be glad to visit the grieving brother."

The lady's eyes pinched at the corners, narrowing. She did not believe Penelope's excuse. And yet, as the day was fine and there were friends to visit, relief smoothed away her worry lines and misgivings. "If it is no bother . . ."

Penelope bent to gather a few mushrooms and hide her expression. With the fungi safely stowed in a tablespoon-sized satchel, she rose and shook her head. "Not in the least."

"Well, then." A folded piece of paper was withdrawn from her handbag. "You will find a list of items I drew up, and here are the funds necessary to purchase them . . ."

When the road branched, they made their farewells and went their separate ways: Mrs Stevenson in search of a cold compress for her throbbing knuckles and Penelope to her offices. For though Grace's death was likely an accident, a tug in her gut, similar to the sensation she had felt when the drakes were upon her, pressed her to, at the very least, meet the brother. After all, what could go wrong?

# CHAPTER 10

## The Chapter with Good Ole Fanny

*"Coelodonta antiquitatis,* colloquially known as
the woolly rhinoceros, has dwelt in England for
millennia. Adaptation has permitted the beasts to
persevere, unlike their cousin, the woolly mammoth,
even in the face of extinction. Namely, their coats
have thinned to accommodate the present climate
of England, Wales, Scotland, and France."

*A Novice's Guide to Flora and Fauna, page 213*

Before visiting the grieving brother, Penelope had an
assistant who needed minding and letters that needed
writing. As Cecilia's Cabinet did not open until midday,
she slipped in the back door, past a waiting Harriet
Greene, the physician's maid, most likely sent in search of
mint or ginger, and quietly climbed the stairs.

The rooms that doubled as her office and Walt's
private residence were silent, which was unsurprising. Walt
often slept past noon. In fact, Penelope would have been
more concerned if she had been awake.

The dim light of the overcast morning filtered through the window. It cast long shadows from the gold-leaf frames across the robin-egg walls. A book lay face down on the chaise, which was a recent addition selected to pair with golden ochre chairs. Penelope righted the novel, placing a calling card to mark the spot. It was a Radcliffe, one that Walt read at least twice a year.

For fun and to pass the time, she perused the naval lists and newspapers, committing the lists of births and the obituaries to memory. An article in *Felix Farley's Bristol Journal* caught her eye. The headline, *Folk Among the Ton,* leapt off the page. Phrases like "Scandalous reports," ". . . reliable source has confirmed that the daughter of Lord — is a sniffer," and "Such untrustworthy persons . . ." led to it being crumpled and tossed onto the dying embers where it belonged. After she organised the remaining papers alphabetically to calm her frazzled nerves, she wrote a dozen notes.

Over the past few years, she had established a network of reliable peddlers of whispered information, otherwise known as gossips. Everyone from the local tavern keeper to members of His Majesty's household gladly answered her letters, sharing the latest news from across England, Wales, and Scotland. Few required coin, as most gladly accepted information as currency instead.

Penelope had found it an effective means of collecting intelligence. After all, why traipse about the countryside when a well-written letter and a tip about the price of coal would yield the same result? It was efficient and easier on her feet.

At one minute past twelve, Walt emerged. Still wearing yesterday's clothes, she flopped into her chair, with feet bare and curled raven hair askew.

Penelope resisted the urge to make a tart comment. Instead, she poured a cup of tea for each of them, adding liberal amounts of sugar to Walt's and a spoonful of honey to her own.

"What are you smiling at?" The assistant cradled her cup with both hands, curling her shoulders forward as though she suspected her employer intended to snatch it from her.

Understanding that sugar and tea possessed a magic of their own, able to transform the snarling ogre before her into a fairly sensible person, Penelope pressed her lips into a line. "'Morning. Your performance yesterday was splendid."

Walt peeked at her from the corner of her eye. "Was it?"

"Yes. I would have thought you had been born the daughter of a country knight had I not known better."

Her words, sincerely meant (and adroitly timed), unruffled Walt's feathers. "Taught by my mum. She was the finest Ophelia of this century, or so said *The Morning Herald*." She reached for the slice of honey cake placed near her chair. Still a tad perturbed, she asked with mock civility, "To what do I owe the pleasure of your company this fine morning?"

{Narrator's Note: Walt was not waxing sentimental. Her dearly departed mother had been a splendid actress. Unfortunately, she was also

72

frequently with child (all girls) and thereby often unemployed. After all, in a society where revealing one's ankles was considered immoral, the sight of a woman with child on stage had naturally been deemed scandalous.}

Penelope eyed the crumbs collecting in her assistant's lap, and withheld a scowl. "Have you time today to visit the taverns and inns along the thoroughfares to enquire after your brother?"

"My brother?" Walt's perfect full lips curled. "I haven't one of—"

Penelope tapped the side of her nose with her finger and winked.

Understanding at last, Walt replied, "Oh! My brother. Yes! He wouldn't happen to be the nameless captain who has recently eloped with Miss Pilkington, would he?" A second cake miraculously appeared on her plate. Three-quarters of it made it into her mouth. The remaining quarter deposited itself in her lap (and on the floor, and on the chair, and on the table).

Unable to restrain herself, Penelope passed her a napkin. "Yes . . ." The urge to gloat urged the corners of her mouth to turn upwards. ". . . and his name is either Captain Charles John Austen or Captain Francis Williams."

"Is it now?" Walt grinned, willing to give praise where praise was due. "And how old is my brother John?"

"Or Francis?"

Having scoffed the last of her breakfast, Walt withdrew her pipe. "Or good ole Franny?"

"Both are thirty or so." She tipped her head towards the book laid across the table. "I have marked pages from archived naval lists that, as his sister . . ." She raised her eyebrows. ". . . you ought to peruse."

"Naturally." Walt nodded. "Why would I gallivant about the country seeking my brother unprotected, though?"

"Let's see . . . You have been seeking new employment, and you wanted to . . ." Penelope waved her hand, inviting Walt to elaborate on the tragic history she had begun to spin.

". . . visit before I begin the position of governess to an earl." Walt hesitated. "On second thought, they may ask which earl. No, a nameless gentleman with two daughters should work."

Penelope twirled the curled hairs near the nape of her neck around her fingers. "Yes, that should do."

Content, Walt sank further into her chair. She savoured the taste of the pipe tobacco, swirling it in her mouth, eyes closed possibly imagining the tale she would spin to best solicit the compassion of tavern keepers and patrons alike. "Damsel in distress is how I'll play it. First, I took the wrong post, and then, I'll have left my reticule on a seat, and then . . ."

While Penelope's ears were attuned to Walt's ramblings, her mind drifted to the case at hand. She considered the web of roadways that crisscrossed the surrounding counties. As Miss Pilkington was of age, she and her beau were unlikely to elope to Scotland. They might flee to the gentleman's home parish. Then again, they might have headed to the coast to—

"Oy! Are you listening?"

"Pardon?" Our sleuth's gaze snapped to her assistant's expression—arms crossed, lips pursed, eyes . . . well, miffed. Penelope slipped a third piece of honey cake onto Walt's plate as a peace offering.

"It doesn't matter." She waved her off. With cake in hand, she went on, "Did you hear? A herd of woolly rhinoceroses *and* field dragons have migrated to Anderson's fields on the north side of the forest."

{Narrator's Note: It has come to the narrator's attention that in some realities, the woolly rhinoceros is extinct. A pity. It is regrettable that other worlds do not know the felicity of spotting a mother with her young or the spectacle of two males sparring. If you do have the opportunity to visit another universe, I highly recommend it.}

"Poor Mr Anderson."

"Bah! The man's a drunkard who has let his field sit fallow these past three years, living off his wife's modest inheritance. Did you not hear the part about the herd?"

"Yes, that would be a sight to see." Penelope checked her watch—nearly half past one. The day was getting away from her; however, it was not every day that a herd of megafauna and dragons ventured near Alderwood. "Did you say they had become one herd?"

"That is what the man at the taproom told me."

"Uncle Archie and I have hypothesised that rhinos and middling dragons have formed an alliance. . ."

She caught Walt's expression. Whenever she waxed poetic about the sciences, or spoke of them in general, a vacant veil would settle over her assistant's face. At times, she wondered whether she had learnt to nap with her eyes open.

Unwilling to disturb abstraction, Penelope rose. She passed through the door to the bedchamber to transform herself into a tradesman's wife. As she sifted through drawers filled with dresses of all conditions, styles, and fabrics, Walt called from the other room. "By the by, how did you do it?"

Penelope suppressed a self-satisfied grin. "Do what, pray tell?"

"None of that false humility, if you please. How'd you discover that Miss Pilkington's fiancé's name was either Captain Charles John Austen or Captain Francis Williams? There must be hundreds of captains in the Royal Navy."

"Simple. I compared the naval lists to ascertain which captains could have visited Cardiff within the last two years, and checked them against those who are ashore at present."

"Lawd," Walt exclaimed. "That must've taken half the morning."

"On the contrary." Penelope selected a sensible dress, shoes, and a spencer, then slipped behind the screen. "As I have memorised the past ten years of naval lists, all that was necessary was a quick perusal of the most recent editions to confirm my suspicions."

"Show-off."

# CHAPTER 11

## The Chapter with the Other Basket

"While the practice of magic is acceptable among
the lower classes, it will never be looked kindly on
by the gentry. The pollution of our noble pedigrees
must not be permitted."

*Sermons to Young Ladies, James Fordyce*

When Penelope arrived at the address provided by Mrs
Stevenson, she did not expect Grace's brother to be home.
After all, a joiner's apprentice could not afford to miss a
day of work, even to grieve for a sister.

Instead, she intended to knock, act surprised when
the landlady verified his absence, insist on delivering the
basket filled with hand pies stuffed with turkey, apples,
potatoes, and turnip, salted meats, and wedges of Double
Gloucester to his room, and then do a bit of snooping. If
she was lucky, she might even manage to leave a window
ajar to permit her to return later.

However, fortune favoured her on this particular
morning. James Sullivan was home. Thankfully, she had
dressed as a respectable tradesman's wife, rather than

Miss Sedgewick of Birch Hallow, who was known far and wide for either her family or her wealth. She had learnt long ago that her title was a barrier to her investigations. No one would confide to a Sedgewick, yet four-fifths of the populace would spill their beans to a Mrs Smith, respectable matron.

Upon her entrance to the third-floor lodgings, three things became apparent.

One, Mr Sullivan was tidier than she would have expected. His lodgings, though humble, were well kept. The wood panelling shone, as did the floors and furniture. Clearly, Grace's brother had applied his skill as a joiner to the upkeep of their chambers.

Two, the young man—not yet twenty, she would hazard—had loved his sister. Though he greeted her with a smile, it did not touch his grey-blue eyes. Sorrow draped itself over him, clouding his expression.

Three, either Grace or her brother were dowsers, as evidenced by the collection of buttons, polished thimbles, and flattened bullets neatly organised by shape and size on the mantel. It resembled her own collection, which she had hidden in a forsaken corner of the attic.

Penelope itched to run her fingers across the items. Oh, what stories they told. Dowsers could not listen to the items they found. No, their abilities were limited to *finding* lost items, as well as sensing when an item had a peculiar tale to tell. She had long considered partnering with a dowser; their combined gifts would be formidable.

She introduced herself and her purpose, after which he offered her a cup of tea, which she gladly accepted. Though he was but seven or eight years younger than her, his boyhood still clung to him. His open face, tanned by the spring sun, was clean-shaven with hints of strawberry-blonde stubble scattered across the cleft of his chin and his upper lip.

"Do allow me to express my sympathies, Mr Sullivan. A loss such as yours is not easy to bear." The words caught in her throat, for though Penelope wore the clothes and habits of Mrs Smith, she still was an orphaned child at heart.

"It's James, and thank you." With care, his calloused hand pulled the kettle from the fire. "I don't know how I will manage without her." He fumbled with the kettle; from nerves or inexperience, she could not tell.

She offered a sympathetic smile and a quiet, "May I?", after which he relinquished the task of preparing the tea to her steady, capable hand. She selected a breakfast tea from the basket she had delivered and spooned it into the pot. "Have your parents been informed?"

The young man had settled into his chair and looked away. "We lost our parents last autumn. Influenza. Grace was away, working. She never even had a chance to say her goodbyes."

Her eye drifted to the hooks near the door—two coats, his and hers. At the far end of the room, two beds peeked from behind a divider. And, by the fire, two chairs sat, angled towards one another.

As a change of subject was in order, she redirected the conversation to Grace. "Yes, I had heard that she had recently returned to Alderwood. From Cirencester, if I remember correctly."

Penelope had not the foggiest idea where his sister's last post might have been. She had learnt that while people grew suspicious when questioned, they were eager to correct an error.

He stared into the hearth, watching the embers dance. "Worcester. Was employed by Lord and Lady Pembroke."

At the clatter of china, he turned.

"How clumsy of me." She righted the toppled cup, mopping up the spilt brown liquid with a rag. After a conciliatory grin, James turned towards the fire once more.

An intentional breath restored her nerves. "As you were saying, Worcester, not Cirencester. How silly of me." Tea tray in hand, she joined the young man by the fire.

"Think nothing of it." He indicated that he took sugar.

After serving the young man, then herself, Penelope permitted a silence to stretch between them, hoping its discomfort would make him eager to talk. "Tell me about Grace."

James stared into his cup.

"I do apologise. I have been too forward. It is simply that I find that speaking of our departed loved ones can . . ."

". . . soothe our spirits," he finished quietly.

"Yes, it can." Had it not been 1811, and had touching the ungloved hand of a man not been tantamount to a marriage proposal, Penelope would have reached across the spindly table to press his hand. Though it pained her to question him, his mention of Lord and Lady Pembroke had stirred her misgivings.

"Grace was like a mum to me. Not that our own mum was . . ." He trailed off.

"Neglectful."

He shook his shaggy curls, ginger like his sister's. "Not at all, but as she worked long hours at the seamstress's shop, Grace and I were left to tend to ourselves."

Leaning back in the chair, he rested his head. The upturn of his lips into a genuine smile told Penelope that fond visions of his sister danced behind his grey-blue eyes. "One of my earliest memories is of us tramping through the forest in search of berries. She always scrubbed my shirt clean afterwards. 'To hide the evidence,' she would say."

A quiet chuckle escaped Penelope's lips. "She sounds like a good older sister."

"She was." His eye drifted to the sewing basket resting near Penelope's feet. "After our parents passed away, she applied to the Abbey, and elsewhere too. Wanted to come home to keep my house, she said." He paused. "I wish she hadn't."

Silence stretched between them—not an uncomfortable one, mind you. It held her unspoken condolences and his thanks. He coughed, clearing his throat. "Not to be disrespectful to Lady Pilkington, you understand. They have been more than kind. They sent her wages, a month's worth. Very generous."

"Indeed." And it was.

Her eyes drifted to the mantel. The collection of odds and ends called to her. She ought not to ask about them. After all, it was impolite to enquire whether someone possessed a gift . . . "The collection on the mantel, did they belong to her?"

Though he answered, "Yes", the clenching of his jaw and how he immediately rose to gather the tea things indicated that either he told the truth or wished to conceal his own gift.

*Interesting . . . Dowsers are constantly in demand—kept aflush with coin by every banker, business, and lawyer in the country. Why be a maid or a joiner if you possessed such a gift?*

"Thank you for the basket." His tone and the flat line of his lips, though not harsh, indicated he wished her to leave.

"Thank the Ladies of Alderwood Aid Society. I am merely a member." She rose and collected her reticule.

He bowed. "It's the second I received."

"Is it?" Subtly, she scanned the room once more, taking note of the window latch—broken. If she had any intention of investigating the matter further, which she did not, thank you very much, she *could* return the next day to peruse Grace's belongings in private.

"Yes, the other came from . . . One moment." He lifted a card from the sideboard. "The Charity League of Gloucestershire."

Penelope nearly stumbled on the rug, which would have been awkward. "Come again?"

"The Charity League of Gloucestershire, or, at least, that's what my landlady said when she delivered it."

"Oh, yes. I had misheard you before." Outwardly, she was the picture of nonchalance. Inwardly, she considered casting herself across the room and ripping the card from his hand. Too obvious?

She made her goodbyes before she crossed the threshold and descended the stairs. She had barely arrived at the first-floor landing before she felt reasonably certain that Grace's death was not the result of a mishap.

For you see, dear Reader, this conversation uncovered two delicious morsels of interest. First, Lord and Lady Pembroke did not reside in Worcester or Cirencester, nor any other Cester within 75 miles. The esteemed Lord Pembroke's estate was in the south-east corner of England. Therefore, either Grace had hidden the identity of her former employer or her brother had. Which could have been dismissed if it had not been for the other basket.

The Charity League of Gloucestershire had not visited young James. As no such organisation existed, it could not have delivered the other basket. So, then, who had?

# CHAPTER 12

## The Chapter with the Megafauna

"According to the testimony of a dozen psychometrists, contact is not necessary to "listen" to the histories imbued in objects of magical origin (dragon scales, unicorn hairs, and the like). Nonetheless, it has been reported that the visions are more vivid and may be accompanied by sounds and smells. However, as Folk are infamous for their deceit, this committee has shelved the matter."

*An Archived Report from the House of Commons Committee on the Regulation of Magical Creatures and Magickind, 1796*

As her aunt was decidedly against keeping a dragon, Penelope had rented a magicked carriage from a local stables instead. A herd of rhinoceroses and field dragons was uncommon and, therefore, warranted the expenditure. Besides, Mr Montagu's aunt' estate lay between Alderwood and the purported location of the herd. Penelope reasoned that if she hired a dragon-drawn carriage, the detour would add no more than ninety minutes to her schedule.

Of course, she could have taken one of the public coaches that connected scattered towns to one another, providing safe transport; however, as ladies never travelled by post without a chaperone, she decided against it. As every lady knows, chaperones rob subterfuge of its fun.

As her arrival drew near, she thought she might have embarked on a fool's errand. The beasts might have moved on, after all.

They had not.

No sooner had they emerged from a copse of sweet-chestnut trees than the carriage came to a halt. Penelope lowered her window to peek up the road. There, in a patch of dappled shade in the middle of the lane, lay a shaggy rhinoceros.

The beast could not be bothered to lift its head at their approach, let alone move. Not one to make a fuss, Penelope alighted from the carriage and instructed the driver to anticipate her return within the hour.

Beyond the hedges of wild berry bushes against a patchwork of farms rose thirty-odd mounds of scales and fur. With as much haste as her dress and her station would permit, she approached, a hum of expectation sizzling in her veins. Had it not been for the presence of half a dozen onlookers milling about, she would have hiked up her dresses past her knees.

The herd was evenly split between the megafauna and dragonkind, with one calf and one hatchling among the cows and she-dragons. Calving season had ended; therefore, the males had long since been banished, left to wander the moors and highlands in solitude. With not a predator in sight and no bothersome males to distract them, the ladies fed on the grasses and wild-flowers or sunned themselves, their eyes shut against the midday rays.

Neither species was bothered by Penelope's approach, though the mothers did bend their heads in her direction. She angled her bonnet so it would shield her eyes against the blinding reflections of the scales.

Though she enjoyed the occasional peek, regularly listening to magical objects had been known to lead to overindulgence. Though even non-Folk could catch fleeting glimpses of the memories of dragon scales or unicorn horns, a listener could plunge headlong into a vision without making contact.

"Glorious, are they not?"

Penelope was not startled, not one bit. The yelp she stifled was the natural reaction to stumbling over a man crouching low in the grass like a drake ready to pounce and nothing more.

"They are." She righted her bonnet and assumed a ladylike posture. "Especially that one there." Her hand gestured towards a wheat-coloured dragon whose horns had begun to curl into spirals. "She must be nearly a hundred and sixty years old."

When the man rose to his feet, she recognised him instantly—Mr Montagu in the flesh—raven hair, crystal-blue eyes, and a jawline that could cut glass. Despite his pleasing appearance, her abdomen constricted in a manner she could not describe as pleasant.

"Closer to two hundred, I would hazard." As he tore his gaze from the herd, recognition dawned in his eyes. He bowed. "Miss Sedgewick."

"Mr Montagu." She curtseyed. Niceties had to be observed, after all. "And I disagree. She cannot be a day above one hundred and sixty. Note her horns: there are merely two turns, not three, and as she is only slightly larger than the rhinoceroses, she cannot yet be two hundred."

"Of course." He grinned the grin of a man who believed he was correct yet thought his partner unequal to grasping the nuances of the subject at hand. In other words, he thought her, and her sex as a whole, stupid. "Lovely day. Is it not?"

It was, or it had become so once the clouds had scattered, revealing an expanse of blue, but she would not admit as much. Had not Penelope sworn she would not draw her pistol unless it were a matter of life and death (and, no, irritating gentlemen did not constitute a mortal threat), Mr Montagu might have suffered an early demise. She imagined how simple a matter the concealment of the shooting would be. Nature would lend a hand. For though field dragons were generally herbivores, they had been known to partake of the occasional stray deer or unfaithful husband. Certainly, were they to discover a recently deceased Englishman near their napping spot, they would devour him whole.

Instead, she did what generations of ladies had done before her: she swore that one day she would humiliate him publicly.

The vision of the calf chasing the hatchling across the field dragged her mind from darker (though enjoyable) daydreams. It was, after all, foolish not to seize the opportunity she had been afforded—to converse with the gentleman away from the prying eyes of others. She forced an airy laugh. "Have you been to town lately?"

"Yes. I dined at the Abbey last week after a day of shooting with Sir Lawrence."

*Oh! Did you?* Her mouth practically salivated at his words. "I trust that Mrs Pilkington and Miss Pilkington are well?"

The fractional dip of the corner of his mouth sent Penelope's heart aflutter. Oh, how she loved it when men emoted involuntarily. Unintentional frowns and eye flutters were such fun to analyse.

"They are well. Miss Pilkington and I sang a duet." He paused, observing a rhino with fur the colour of burnt umber scratch its shoulder against her neighbour's hooked armour. For her impertinence, the half-slumbering dragon swatted the libertine with her tail. "Have you had the pleasure of hearing her sing, or play, for that matter?"

She had, but as she wished to observe rather than persuade, her sole reply was a shake of her head.

Mr Montagu chuckled at the sight of the hatchling and calf sparring. "It is a true delight. She has the voice of an angel."

Our heroine, in a display of herculean restraint, did not roll her eyes at the cliche. Ugh! It was no wonder female megafauna and dragonkind forced their males to wander alone.

The approach of a man and woman caused a stir among the herd. They wore plainer clothes, he in a brown coat and she in a straw bonnet embellished by a woven ribbon and wildflowers. She held a bouquet in her hand.

"What are they playing at?" Taking his hat off, Mr Montagu waved it to gain their attention. However, his attempt went unheeded.

As the woman stepped nearer, a curious yearling, whose scales' colour shifted like ripe wheat in the wind, tilted her head. The young woman chuckled when the dragon bounded across the waist-high grasses to greet her.

Though Mr Montagu's face indicated that he had not yet comprehended, Penelope understood—the pair, or at least the girl, were Folk: a whisperer, she would hazard. Her suspicions were confirmed when the girl extended her hand to scratch the dragon under her chin before they turned and walked side by side, the man trailing behind them.

"Scourge of polite society." Mr Montagu muttered. Disgust contorted his pleasing features." I, for one, was against the Magic Act. Weren't you?" Unaware that he had stepped out of a hornet's nest only to land in a drake's den, he flashed her a smile.

"Yes." She pursed her heart-shaped mouth, permitting a grin that even pixies would have labelled as wicked. "It was a poorly written law that legalized magic without properly appreciating its potential. The consequences were the predation of those with money on those in need of it and the repression of magic among the gentry, depriving society of their talents." Penelope forced a girlish giggle. "Do you not agree?"

Mr Montagu, sensible of his adversary's standing (or that he was out of his depth), bowed. "Of course."

Convinced that the field dragons *would* enjoy a Montagu-flavoured treat if she remained a moment longer, she plotted her escape. Beyond the field, at the edge of the wood, she had spied a cottage—or at least she suspected that a cottage lay underneath the hill of herbs, wild English roses, and twisted vines. It was likely the home of an herbalist or a nurturer. Both were known for their hospitality, especially if one purchased a salve or tincture as a thanks.

She drew her handkerchief from her reticule, careful not to dislodge her spare dagger, and patted her décolleté.

The gentleman (in name only) noticed. "Miss Sedgewick, you will become faint if you remain in the sun a moment longer. You must permit me to escort you to your carriage."

{Narrator's Note: Reader, it was not warm, not in the least. In fact, on the second of April in the year 1811, the temperature peaked at what most people would call pleasant. And, though pleasant is not strictly a scientific term, you get the point.}

"Thank you for your . . ." *not-so-subtle attempt to rid yourself of my presence* ". . . attentions, but I believe I shall nip into the cottage first. It is not far, and I feel equal to the task. Besides, perhaps I can persuade its inhabitant to fetch me a cool glass of cucumber water."

"Are you certain? It is no trouble."

"Do not think on it a moment longer. I am sure I shall find the walk restorative."

Her curtsey announced her intention of departing. And his bow proclaimed that he was glad to be rid of her.

# CHAPTER 13

## The Chapter with the Pirate Cat

"Rather have a cat as a guard, I would. More
reliable than men, and cheaper, too."

*Mrs Oleander White, Healer*

After dodging a rabbit hole or two and the afternoon
coach to Alderwood, Penelope crossed the packed dirt lane
bordering the wood.

Before her, rising from hills of wildflowers, was a
cottage that had tumbled out of a fairytale. Every nook
of the garden that was not packed with herbs and vines
contained fairy houses, green men, and geodes. When
she grasped the cracked paint of the kissing gate, she
envisioned a half-hour to herself, sipping tea and wrestling
with her misgivings.

"What'd you want?" called a voice. Framed by the
arched doorway stood the nurturer, whose ice-white
hair tumbled down her shoulders to her waist like an
avalanche. Her sharp eye darted from Penelope to Mr
Montagu in the distance.

Sensing that before her stood no willowy fairy-chaser, Penelope lifted her chin. "A cup of tea, if you would be so kind . . ."

Distracted as she was by the woman's brisk manner (and the field mouse peering out from the pocket of her apron), she had failed to notice the figure of a slender girl standing in the doorway behind her. With a scowl that could have reformed the Prince Regent, the woman stepped in front of the girl, blocking her from Penelope's view.

The healer jutted her chin forward. "My apprentice."

Penelope acknowledged the girl with a curtsey. "Also, would you happen to have a salve for eczema and a tincture for fatigue?"

Just as she had hoped, the quick coin the healer would earn from the tincture put her in a more hospitable mood. Ingredients to relieve fatigue were rare and, therefore, demanded a pretty penny. For Penelope, such a payment was a pittance compared to the solace a cup of tea would provide.

"Will the gentleman be joining you?" The elder woman spat the word 'gentleman' as though it were a curse.

Penelope shook her head. "As I have only just escaped his attentions, I hope not."

A flash of mischievousness brightened the woman's face. "That much of a bother, was he?

She leaned in. "Worse."

"Right this way. Healer Sable is at your service." The pair weaved down a path that appeared to be at war, threatened by the onslaught of peppermint, lemon balm, and fennel.

"Thank you, Mrs Sable."

"Save your 'misses' and 'mistresses' for another, if you please."

Never in her life had Penelope been so enchanted by chaos. Jutting out of the waves of lush herb plants rose a jollyboat turned flower box. Under the nurturer's hand, jasmine had woven itself into a sail. The crow's nest was manned by a slumbering raccoon.

She could almost taste magic in the air—conjured not by humankind but by Mother Nature's own hand. It would not have surprised her in the least to discover a unicorn resting among the marigolds and daffodils.

As they continued, the faint odour of metal and the urge to sneeze alerted Penelope to the proximity of several talismans. A polished riverstone hung from the woman's neck, likely containing a charm to ward off enemies. Though finicky and prone to backfiring, they were useful charms for those who nursed feuds.

It was, however, the aquamarine geodes (thief-thwarters perhaps) posted at intervals throughout the garden that forced Penelope to pluck a couple of lemon verbena leaves as they delved deeper into the wilderness. She crushed them between her fingers to release the oils before brushing the scent across her upper lip. The bold odour quieted the pressing desire to sneeze. An errant "Achoo!" would have drawn Sable's already watchful eye.

"Here we are, miss." Roots and vines coaxed into a natural gazebo were evidence of her skill as a master nurturer. Even the tables and stools were alive.

An involuntary sigh escaped Penelope's lips. "It is lovely."

The furrows that lined the woman's cheeks deepened as she grinned. "Much appreciated. I shall return with your tea."

Penelope reclined in a chair of wisteria branches. She exhaled. This was a place without schedules or appointments, where time faded like the morning mist. Days and hours were marked by the sunrise and sunsets, the buds of spring, and the ripening fruit, not by calendars or watches. Peace infused Penelope's skin, soaking into her bones.

Her mind drifted to Rose Pilkington and Grace Sullivan. Two women whose lives could not be more dissimilar. One had known luxury, while the other had scrubbed her hands until they cracked and bled to earn her bread. While Grace's evenings were spent serving others, Rose danced with—

A rustling of leaves at the far end of the gazebo distracted her. From a knot of vines emerged a tawny cat with a patch of black fur framing its right eye. The feline reminded Penelope of a pirate. "What ho, Sir Sentry. Is this your garden?"

He bent his head, indicating that it was his garden and she had not submitted the proper paperwork to gain entry. He leapt onto the second chair to appraise the trespasser.

"I do apologise for not introducing myself sooner. I am Miss Sedgewick. How do you do?"

Aware that before him stood no ruffian, the cat answered her with a bow. Always prepared, Penelope fished a sprig of dried catnip from her reticule. The impudent scallywag winked at her when she placed it on the table.

"Charmer."

He bobbed his head and then lounged in the chair in a pose reminiscent of Blackbeard himself.

"As you have interrupted my internal dialogue, the gentlemanly thing to do would be to listen as I weigh my options." She raised her eyebrows, awaiting an answer.

The cat shrugged.

A nod sufficed as thanks. "To summarise, yesterday, I discovered the body of a deceased maid. At first glance, there was nothing more scandalous than dust at the scene."

Both the cat and the lady scrunched their noses in disgust.

"I know. There is no evidence of foul play, and even if there were, the parish constable would not waste his time investigating the murder of a maid." Penelope rose to pace back and forth.

"And yet, I cannot ignore this . . ." She clenched her hands into fists. ". . . knowledge, no, certainty that there is more to the matter than meets the eye."

An expression she could only interpret to mean, *Perhaps it is a human thing, but I do not understand. Investigate the matter if you are so inclined,* crossed her furry companion's face.

Penelope reclaimed her seat. "I could, but . . ." She leaned across the table, careful not to crush the puffball fungi sprouting as a centrepiece. ". . . I have never looked into a matter as grave—"

Her confessor rolled his yellow eyes.

"Pardon the pun." She winked. "As I was saying, I have never taken on a matter as dire as this. Thefts? Easy. Philandering husbands? I call that Monday. Missing persons? Less common, but simple. Yet this, dear friend . . . We are friends now, aren't we?"

Her potential friend had the decency to cease cleaning his paws to dip his chin as confirmation.

"If I were to learn that Grace had been killed, how would I bring her killer to justice without disclosing my alternative persona? Or worse—"

Penelope would have continued. In fact, she might have bared her soul, confessed her gifts, and spilt the beans about a certain Duke who had taken up with . . . Well, a secret that salacious will cost you. However, her eye caught the apprentice's approach, weaving her way through the garden and bearing a tray of tea with a jar of honey.

"We have never met," she mumbled as she placed a second sprig at his feet. Before the girl had drawn near, he had taken it in his mouth and disappeared into the tangled ocean of plants once more.

A few moments passed before the pit-pat of bare feet announced the girl's arrival. The girl averted her gaze and hunched her shoulders as though she wished to sink into the earth. Without a word, she placed the tray on the table.

Between the charm wrapped around the delicate teapot (to prevent cracking or theft) and the other worn by the apprentice, Penelope could no longer contain herself. She burst forth with a resounding "Achoo!" Her sneeze was so powerful that three dragons and two rhinoceroses turned to discover the source of the ruckus.

"I beg your pardon," she apologised.

The girl merely curtseyed before she vanished into the snarled vine archways once more.

After half an hour and a pot of tea, Penelope emerged from the garden, her purchases in tow. As she stepped up into her carriage and instructed the driver to deliver her to Lady Montagu's estate, she paused and turned to catch a glimpse of the herd once more. The woolly rhinoceros who had blocked their path had moved on, as must she.

# CHAPTER 14

## The Chapter with the Sugar

"Tinctures, salves, and balms cannot be detected by
a sniffer and, therefore, are easier to conceal."

*A Healer's Guide to Gardening, page 214*

"And to what do I owe the pleasure of your company this
fine spring day?"

Tempted as Penelope was to answer, "Your nephew's
impending heartbreak," she did not. Honesty was rarely
the best policy, especially when surreptitiously questioning
aunts.

An afternoon gallivanting about the countryside
in quest of megafauna preceded by a morning spent
escaping predatory dragons had left our heroine famished.
Therefore, when Lady Montagu's butler presented
Penelope with a tray of cold meats, aged cheeses, and
seed cake, it took all of her self-possession not to fall on
it like a dragon snacking on a would-be viscount. Instead,
she accepted the wafer-thin porcelain adorned with
faedragons and yellow roses, thanked her, and nibbled
with as much delicacy as she could muster.

As honey had not been offered, Penelope was forced to wash down the dry cheeses with a sip of black tea, unsweetened. Blech! "As I have not had the pleasure of calling upon you since January, I felt that an effort was long overdue."

"You went to see the woolly rhinoceros and dragon herd, did you?" The naughty sexagenarian smirked. Though her face was square and her appearance plain, Penelope had long regarded Lady Montagu as handsome. Her features were average—a middling nose, unremarkable lips, and a pronounced brow suggesting her family heralded from the east—yet her determination lent them a beauty that could not be contained in a charm.

"Do not fret, my dear. When I was your age, I visited my neighbours out of a sense of duty as well. Think nothing of it. I am glad for the company."

Lady Montagu's directness was as legendary as her scone recipe. To a young lady plagued by conversations with less depth than a teaspoon, Penelope found her hostess's earnestness refreshing. She desperately hoped that her call would not only further her investigation but also expose her to Lady Montague's scandalous opinions, which, though not proper, were often correct.

Their conversation wafted from the woolly rhinoceroses to the startling increase in yeti sightings. As the estate had recently been redecorated, Penelope turned the conversation in that direction, hoping to steer it nearer Mr Montagu.

"This room is lovely." She admired the bold colour choice. Midnight-blue paint had been applied to the walls, door frames, doors, and even the moulding. The cerulean and pinkish violets in the drapes and furnishing contrasted with the sombre tone, producing an effect she could only describe as striking. And the ceiling had been painted to resemble a moonless night sky.

"I find it enlivening." Her sixty-two-year-old eye caressed the charcoal rug embellished with vibrant chrysanthemums, each the width of a man's stride. "As does Lord Montagu."

"Without a doubt, Mr Montagu appreciates your efforts." Penelope prodded.

"Bah!" Lady Montagu's eyes nearly disappeared into her pronounced eyebrows when she rolled them. She leaned forward, a bemused expression enlightening her features. "My husband's nephew loathes it."

The younger woman raised her teacup—a toast to her cunning. "Does his lordship's nephew intend to prolong his visit here?"

Lady Montagu sighed. "You have heard about his intentions towards Miss Pilkington, then, have you?"

"Who has not?"

"Ha!" Her ladyship slapped her knee before reclining against the buttery pillows piled high around her. "Not a living soul this side of London, I would imagine."

After a cursory glance to ensure that the door was firmly closed, she continued, "Between you and me, his intentions do not suit, and I would rather he left the girl well alone."

*Oh, really?* Penelope's eyebrows shot into her hairline.

"None of your brow raises, young miss." Though her hand remained in her lap, she wagged a finger disapprovingly. "She has about as much common sense as a hen, and yet she is unspoilt, whereas my nephew . . ."

Her eye darted to the last cake, then caught her guest's eye. Taking the hint, Penelope transferred the cake from the serving tray to the lady's plate—a bribe of sorts.

Satisfied, Lady Montagu elaborated. "Well, he is a man of the world with certain . . . tastes, which a young lady like herself cannot satisfy."

Had it not been for years of studying the art of self-possession, Penelope would have spat an unsweetened mouthful of tea across the rug like a fountain cherub. Instead, she sputtered, eliciting a grin from the Viscountess.

"Perhaps, then . . ." The corners of Penelope's lips stayed put so as not to betray the gossip she was about to divulge. ". . . it is providential that Miss Pilkington has gone to visit her cousin."

"Has she? Interesting." The lady's deep inset eyes were ablaze with curiosity. "Not at all what I would expect from a young lady intent on snagging a future viscount."

"I hear they are nearly sisters, and she felt compelled to be at her side to help care for her first child. Or so I have heard." Penelope had heard no such thing, but experience had taught her that details sell a story.

"Naturally." As Lady Montagu leaned forward to take a wedge of aged cheddar, she winced. "Old age. It is a literal pain in my . . . Well, everywhere."

Penelope accepted her hostess's plate from her outstretched hand, piling it high with the cheeses and meats she had observed her select at the start of her visit.

Once it had been settled on her lap once more, Lady Montagu said, "It is just as well. When he hears of her departure, his interest will turn elsewhere, and both Miss Pilkington and I will be better for it."

The insinuation of the Viscountess's words was not lost on our sleuth. *So, she will be glad when he departs. Perhaps I should take my time in discovering Miss Pilkington to allow her ample time to wed her captain.*

During her abstraction, her hostess had refilled their respective cups. "Sugar?"

She lifted the cup and saucer to her lap and shook her head.

"Oh, I do apologise. You take honey in your tea, do you not?" She added a teaspoon of sugar to her drink. "I would like to blame it on old age, but even as a young woman, I found my skills as a hostess labelled deficient. Speaking of sugar, I read the most fascinating article about its health benefits . . ."

While the lady expounded on the virtues of sugar, Penelope felt suspended in time. Her mind transported her back to the parlour of the Abbey, to Grace splayed across the hearth. That was it—the persistent question her mind could not ignore. Where was the sugar bowl?

Half a dozen calls had taught her that the Pilkingtons took sugar with their tea. So, why had there been no sugar bowl on the tray—no sugar crystals embedded in the rug? And for that matter, both the mother and daughter preferred milk, and yet the dried tea in the cup did not contain a drop.

In her mind's eye, she pictured the room. It rose before her. There, across the rug, lay the pot with its lid, a teacup, a saucer, a spoon, and a creamer—but no bowl.

And the body . . . It was the amount of tea spilt on the apron that had felt unnatural.

"Drat!"

The Lady Montagu started.

"I apologise for my outburst. Though this is terribly rude of me, will you excuse me?" Hushing the torrent of excitement mixed with shame, Penelope smoothed her dress as she rose. "I have recalled a pressing matter in need of my attention."

Her ladyship shrugged, puffing out her bottom lip. "Of course, my dear. Do not let me detain you. Lord knows I could use a nap. "

Without rushing, not even one bit (though her cup did clatter as she returned it to the tray, eliciting a wince from her hostess), Penelope pressed the elder woman's hand and made her goodbyes.

"Send my regards to your uncle and aunt." Lady Montagu called after her as she all but ran from the room. "Persuade them to call on me if you are so inclined. I find their conversation diverting."

# CHAPTER 15

## The Chapter with All the Pushing

"An object at rest stays at rest, and an object in motion stays in motion with the same speed and in the same direction unless acted upon by an unbalanced force."

*Sir Isaac Newton*

Though the staff of Birch Hallow universally agreed that Miss Sedgewick had burst into the manor that Sunday evening, she had not. The door had stuck, so yes, she *had* pushed it open, but that was *not* bursting, not in the least.

Regardless, the shuddering of the oak doors slamming against the frame drew Uncle Archie's (and a couple of resident ghosts') attention. His head, along with his windstorm-inspired hairstyle, popped into the hall. He signed, "Is that you shaking the house?"

"I have no idea what you are referring to." She let the footman take her reticule and bonnet. "Come with me!"

He fell into step beside her, his hands excitedly forming a question, "Off to make mischief, then, are we?"

"No."

Dear Uncle Archie's expression fell. One would have thought he had been informed that the earth was not an irregularly shaped ellipsoid but a perfect sphere.

She took his hand and kissed it. "Something better. We have a hypothesis to test."

Half an hour later, three mattresses, one chalkboard, and a maid's uniform had been delivered to the parlour.

With her uncle's aid, Penelope recreated the precise layout of the Pilkingtons' parlour, paying particular attention to the rug's proximity to the desk and the fireplace.

"Remind me why it was necessary to swap the rugs," her uncle huffed as he scooted the canapé a quarter of an inch.

"Accuracy, uncle, accuracy. That, and I am rather fond of the other rug."

{Narrator's Note: She was not fond of the rug. In fact, she did not give two figs about it. She would have filled the entire ballroom with tea to test her theory. No, the rug had been switched because the original one was too thick. In order to replicate Grace's death as near perfectly as possible, she had to find a substitute.}

Penelope stepped into a side room to don an apron resembling the one worn by Grace. As she hung her spencer on a knob, a folded piece of paper fell to the floor with a clap.

"Blast!"

There, rumpled and decidedly not delivered, lay her uncle's letter. Between the romp through the forest, the call to James, Grace's brother, the detour to view the herd, and the tea with Lady Montagu, she had forgotten to deliver it.

"Penelope——" Her uncle, who had stepped into the room, stopped. He glanced at the letter, then at her, revelation spreading across his face.

"Uncle, I apologise. I forgot——"

"No need to apologise." Though his expression was warm, the mirthful glimmer had vanished from his eye. He lifted the letter from the floor, stuffing it into the pocket of his rumpled coat. "It was foolish of me to have you deliver them all this time."

The tightness in her chest threatened to rob her of breath. For ten years, she had faithfully delivered his letters to the box in the woods, until today. "Uncle——"

His hands covered hers, silencing her. He shook his head, and released her fingers to sign. "I shall deliver it myself tomorrow."

Even though she had left childhood behind some years before, she felt in that moment like the little girl who had once spilt tea across her uncle's most cherished almanac.

He tucked his knuckle under her chin and lifted it. "None of that. We have a hypothesis to test."

Two maids, the butler, the housekeeper, and one footman entered bearing five trays, each holding one teapot of hot tea, one creamer, one spoon, and one cup and saucer. As the staff had grown accustomed to the Sedgewicks' peculiarities, none batted an eye as they placed them on a bench near the window. The housekeeper was the last to exit, careful to close the door behind her.

Uncle Archie clapped. "Tell me, my dear, of your hypothesis."

He crossed the room to the blackboard. Faint traces of former theorems and formulas clung to it still.

"It is my theory that a . . ." *shoved victim* ". . . a shove will accelerate the velocity of a fall."

He transcribed her words in a cramped hand. "A sound theory. A push certainly would alter the axis of rotation."

"Of course." Having donned the maid's apron, she carried a tray to the desk. Though she was shorter than Grace, she would have to do.

"Furthermore . . ." The comforting tap-tap, tap-tap of the chalk against the board put Penelope at ease. "The path of the center of mass would change dramatically."

She lifted the tray. "Precisely." Before she stepped backwards, she stomped on the floor to draw her uncle's attention. He turned, having felt the vibration, then laid his chalk aside and moved near the mattress propped against the fireplace.

"Observe." She stepped back. Her heel caught against the rug. Involuntarily, she released the tray. It tipped forward as her left foot stepped back in an attempt to right her. Soon, two firm hands caught her, preventing her from crashing into the fireplace.

Once standing on her two feet, Penelope glanced down at her uniform. The teacup had splattered across her apron, yet the rug bore the worst of the stains.

"The lid!" Uncle Archie pointed. "It remained in position until the pot had tipped at an angle greater than ninety degrees."

She collected the pot, which had survived, and knelt to gather the remains of the cup. "Of course, the stopper would have prevented it from falling prematurely."

{Narrator's Note: For those not familiar with the anatomy of a teapot, the stopper is an L-shaped knob on the inside of the lid. It exists to keep the lid in place when the tea is poured. Cheers!}

With the pot in hand and lid in place, she tipped it. When the spout had angled towards the earth, the stopper caught the lid momentarily before it fell with a thump onto the mattress.

Uncle Archie hurried to the blackboard to record his observations. He paused. "As it is outside the scope of our experiment today, we need not measure the precise angle, but I would estimate that the lid became dislodged at an angle of about one hundred and ten degrees."

While he finished his notes, Penelope poked her head into the hall. She called to a passing footman, "Excuse me, Tom. Please step in for a moment?"

The young man entered the parlour. Though he was a recent addition to the staff, he had experienced enough within the first month of his employ to be familiar with the household's peculiarities.

"Welcome, Tom." Uncle Archie greeted him with a grin. As he had not yet sufficient time to learn more than the most basic signs, Penelope interpreted by giving voice to her uncle's signs and signs to the footman's words. "So, will you be the pusher or the catcher?"

Poor Tom looked as though he had encountered one of the fae rather than been asked a simple question. "I beg your pardon, Sir?"

"Push or catch? Really, it is quite simple."

The young man continued to stare.

Uncle Archie turned to his niece, confused. "Are you voicing it correctly? He looks as though he is having a fit."

"Likely, he does not wish to lose his position." Her aunt's formidable figure draped in black muslin stood framed in the doorway. She stepped into the room. "You may go, Tom."

The footman disappeared faster than a final slice of plum pudding.

{Narrator's Note: Yes, Aunt Josephine is adorned in black and has been for nearly thirty years. As the author does not wish to disclose her backstory at this juncture and may not have even nailed down the particulars herself, we must wait.}

Penelope and Uncle Archie, realising the error of their ways, stared at their shoes. It had been wrong of them to involve a male staff member in their experiments. His gran would have whacked him on the head with a pan if word got out that he had shoved, or caught for that matter, Miss Sedgewick. The pair shuffled their feet, prepared to suffer Aunt Josephine's wrath.

"So . . ." Aunt Josephine rolled up her sleeves. "Who needs pushing?" She signed. Glee glimmered in her crystal eyes as she turned to her brother. "Do tell me it is you, dear brother, that I shall have the pleasure of shoving."

The twinkle in Uncle Archie's hazel eyes reflected her own delight. "No. I will be the catcher."

"If you must." Aunt Josephine followed her niece to the desk.

Penelope took her position near the edge of the rug, a fresh tray in hand. "We are observing how the force of a push alters the arc of a fall. If static friction—"

Without so much as a glimmer of mischievousness to warn her, Aunt Josephine shoved her niece—hard. The tray fell from Penelope's hands as she became a tangle of fabric and limbs. And though her uncle caught her, preventing serious injury, his back collided with a thud against the wall beside the mantel.

No sooner had she regained her footing than he brushed past her. "Well done," he said, shaking his sister's hand. "She did not suspect it in the least."

The brother and sister crossed to the blackboard while Penelope checked that all of her limbs were intact. Uncle Archie began to scribble a complex formula measuring arc.

"Don't forget to factor in the force of gravity, Archibald."

"I was just getting to that."

The two vacillated between complimenting and badgering each other. While they focused on the algebra, Penelope observed the scene.

In both scenarios, the tray had tipped forward, preventing the lion's share of the tea from soiling her apron. Her mind pictured the scene in the Pilkingtons' parlour.

How had she not noted it before? Tea had not been spilt on poor Grace; it had been poured. Her misgivings should not only have been piqued by the sheer volume, but by the splatter across the underside of Grace's chin. A novice mistake. Penelope inwardly vented a string of very naughty words, which, if the author were to record them, would instantly have her books banned from most reading circles.

"Penelope! Are you listening?"

She turned to see her aunt staring at her. "No. Please say it once more."

While her uncle erased half of the board in a huff, her aunt observed her demeanour—eyes tight, mouth pinched. "Are you alright, dear?"

A passable smile was plastered on Penelope's face. "Of course." She untied the soiled apron and joined them. "Please do go on."

Her aunt began to rattle off a string of questions about her experience. Uncle Archie continued to scribble various Latin and Greek letters. And Penelope hushed the sinking sensation in her gut—indigestion, of course, and nothing more.

# CHAPTER 16

## The Chapter with Frank the Footman

"The day is gone, the night's our own,
Then let us feast the soul;
If any care or pain remain,
Why, drown it in the bowl."

*Drown it in the Bowl - A Ballad*

Three hours and a quick rinse later, Penelope passed through Cecilia's Cabinet once again. Two hours of being repeatedly shoved, tripped, and bathed in tea had left her sore. It was splendid.

Yes, she had bruised her tailbone and ruined the rug, but the exercise had assured her that she was correct; Grace had been murdered, and an inhabitant of the Abbey had had a hand in disguising her death as an accident.

A quick stop at the counter made Penelope the owner of a vanity charm, one so complex she sneezed twice before entering the back hall. Once the charm had been safely stowed in a containment satchel, she ascended the stairs.

Contrary to her expectations, Walt was not out. Instead, Penelope discovered her draped across a chair, her legs dangling over the arm.

"Whatchoo doin' here?" Her pipe bobbed in her mouth.

"I could ask the same of you." With no time for dilly-dallying, Penelope crossed to the chest to seek a fitting disguise. Drawers of dresses were opened and shut with such haste that the perfume bottles resting atop the cabinet shook. "Should you not be seeking your . . ." She winked. ". . . dear brother?"

"Franny will keep." She craned her neck to better observe Penelope. "And whatchoo winking for? No one's here. And we both know its cover story. Besides, I have visited half the inns and taverns bordering Alderwood. I even popped into a nanny house."

Penelope withdrew a pair of sensible stockings before stepping into the doorway. "A bordello?"

Walt shrugged. "Who knows? Ole Franny may have had a few wild oats that needed sowing."

Behind the shade in the bedroom, Penelope stripped to her shift. While she slipped into a slate-hued dress made of a hardy fabric, she marvelled at her assistant's intuition. What she lacked in education (and tact, and manners, and . . .), her gut compensated for in spades. Of course a captain on the eve of his nuptials might have stopped by such an establishment for one final hurrah.

With the talisman wedged between her, well, diddies, she doused her neck with rose water before viewing herself in the mirror. She burst into a fit of laughter.

Walt, convinced that her employer had finally gone mad, loped into the room. She did not make a sarcastic remark nor whistle like a drunkard. Instead, she fell to her knees, clutching her side and weeping with delight. "Lord, miss! What sort of investigating have you got planned for tonight?"

Penelope reached for a handkerchief and extended a second to Walt. "The sort that involves loose tongues." Her eyes grew to the size of dinner plates. "Not . . . I did not mean . . . You must not think—"

Even had her assistant wished to hear her explanations, she could not. She rolled on the rug, tears streaming down her face.

Several minutes and three handkerchiefs later, both ladies stood before the mirror, nearly rational creatures once more (not that Walt would permit anyone to call her rational). The vanity charm had lengthened Penelope's eyelashes, rounded her angular face, and transfixed her lips in a perpetual pout. It was the enhancement of her bust, though, that Penelope found most provocative. True, she had stuffed her corset with a pair of stockings and laced it tight. However, the charm worked a magic of its own. Without the charm, her diddies were comparable to hills (and that was being generous). With it, they resembled the Alps.

"Have I overdone it this time?"

"Nah." Walt fastened a button Penelope had missed near her neck. "Just 'cause you look as if you plan to provide certain sorts of entertainment to gentlemen for a profit does not mean it has been overdone."

Penelope grimaced.

"Trust me." She clapped her on the shoulder. "No one, not even your own aunt, will know you."

And they did not. The shopkeeper's assistants did not recognise her as she exited to the street. Her milliner did not know her when he ran into a street lamp while bidding her good day. Even her own coachman did not spot her when he held open the door at the tavern nearest the Pilkington estate.

Bent on observing her employer in the wild, as she put it, Walt had invited herself on the evening's excursion.

Whether it was the effects of the charm or . . . Let us be honest, it was the charm without a doubt. As I was saying . . . the effects of the charm rendered the tavern keeper speechless. All he could muster was a grunt as he welcomed them into the taproom.

Once seated, Walt ordered a rum, and Penelope requested a brandy.

Walt sniggered. "You'll want to aim less for innocent maiden and more for wanton—"

Not even a charm as potent as the one she wore could disguise the blush that crept up Penelope's neck and cheeks.

The taproom was relatively quiet; it was only eight in the evening, after all. Hushed conversation interspersed with bursts of laughter or shouts added a cosiness to the room. Penelope surveyed the faces, recognising all but two.

An inviting scene spread before her. Across the fieldstone fireplace and its rough-hewn mantel, the taproom's mistress had displayed a collection of plates depicting rural scenes. It reflected the quaint atmosphere of the room kept clean by her loving hand.

On the opposite wall hung her husband's pride and joy—an Irish elk rack. It loomed over the room, spanning half the ceiling's width and held aloft by ropes secured to the rafters overhead. Though the owner claimed to have shot the beast, in all reality, it had stumbled into the kitchen and died of fright when he screamed in terror.

{Narrator's Note: It has come to our attention that Irish Elk are also extinct in other realities. A pity. Their antlers are as wide as two men and remarkable to behold.}

With her brandy in hand, she unleashed a coy smile on one of the Abbey's groundskeepers. The poor dolt fell off his chair.

"What are we doing here anyway?" Walt cradled her rum in her hand, swirling the amber liquid.

With a wicked expression on her face (which caused a man at the next table to swoon), Penelope whispered, "Collecting dirt."

"Oh, I do love a good morsel of gossip." Walt pounded the wooden table in delight. "And who might be the subject of our noble efforts?"

"Sir Henry Pilkington."

Walt nodded.

"Mr Montagu."

She dipped her chin.

"And Grace Sullivan."

Her assistant's gaze snapped to meet hers. "Thought we were going to leave that one alone."

Penelope leaned across the table, careful not to spill out of her dress. "We were, but . . ."

It was at that moment that a man with a fine figure and a twinkle in his eye that had doubtlessly melted hundreds of hearts materialised.

Thankfully, Walt caught her employer's signal not to serve him with a black eye for his pertness.

"Good evening, ladies." Oh, he was good. He possessed that rare sort of arrogance that was tempered by charm. Confidence bolstered by dozens of stolen kisses oozed from his pores. "May I?"

Penelope peered at him through her heavy lashes. "Of course."

While the young man ordered another round, she secretly dabbed peppermint oil under her nose to prevent her from sneezing. Knowing she would be wearing a powerful charm, she had brought a full bottle. It was no larger than a halfpenny and could be kept hidden by sleight of hand.

Since Walt's eyes were stuck in a perpetual roll, the man turned his smiles on Penelope. "My name is Frank. And who do I have the pleasure of meeting?"

As an heiress, she bristled at the liberties he had taken by introducing himself in such a manner. As a sleuth parading as a flirt, she could not believe her good fortune. Before her sat Frank the footman, determined flirt and, if the Pilkington's maid's wild conjectures were true, Grace's former lover and possible killer. Delish.

"I am Delilah. Charmed."

He leaned close in a way that only men who knew they were handsome dared. "And what tempts you . . ." He parted his lips invitingly. ". . . to visit this fine establishment this evening?"

She parried his insinuations by tipping her bust forward a fraction of an inch, but only that, as she did not want the man to have a fit. After all, another corpse would be of no use to her, and significantly harder to question.

His eyes dipped before they met hers once again.

"My family lives a good way off," Penelope said, "and I have come to Alderwood to seek a position." A sip of brandy left a droplet on her lip. She brushed it away with her finger, but not before she licked it clean. Poor Frank made a sort of strangling noise in his throat.

Walt kicked her under the table, which she interpreted to mean, *Steady. Even young men have been known to drop dead of a stroke. And I'd prefer not to have to shoot him if he should become too friendly.*

In one gulp, Frank downed the rest of his ale. "It so happens that I work at a nearby estate, and though I've only been there since February, I can recommend you, if you like."

"Really." She leaned in.

"Yes." His little finger brushed against hers.

She pulled her hand away to toy with a tendril curling at the nape of her neck. "And, as a female member of the staff, would I be safe? Or is the master of the house a rake?"

"My own sister is employed there as a maid, so yes, you'd be safe, except . . ." A dimple added even more charm to his face. ". . . from me, if you'd like."

She fluttered her eyes, scandalised. "So the master is a gentleman in name and in conduct?"

"He is." Frank signalled for another ale. "A bit of a flirt, but I haven't heard his name connected with anything untoward."

"And not violent?"

"Has a bit of temper, but nothing to be concerned about. The mistress of the house is often away visiting or drinking tea or whatever fine folk do with their time. They leave the management of the house to the steward and the housekeeper. Both of 'em are alright."

"Perhaps, then, I shall apply." Penelope, who found playing the role of a jade to be quite diverting, flashed the footman a grin. "Though I did hear recently of a maid who had been found dead nearby. It does cause me concern. Perhaps I should seek a position in town instead."

Frank took her hand into his. He brushed his lips across her knuckles. "I'd personally guarantee your safety." Had he been whispering the first dozen digits of pi to her, she would have been a lost woman, but as he likely had never even heard of the word radius, his smiles were wasted.

Walt shifted her position, moving near to the cup at Frank's elbow. To distract the poor lad, Penelope twirled a curl with her fingers. "So you did not know her then?"

"I did, but not well. She fell, nothing more." He downed a swig of ale, transfixed by the pout of her lips— not exactly the behaviour of a man who had murdered a former fling.

Aware that had the young man any rumours to share, he would have done so, Penelope shifted the conversation towards Alderwood.

As expected, within about three minutes, poor Frank's eyes became unfocused. Another minute more, and his head landed with a thud on the table.

"Held out longer than I expected, that one." Walt rose, knocking back the last dregs of her drink.

"A man of that weight and height generally takes about four minutes to feel the effects of a sleeping draught." Penelope left her drink unfinished and departed for the door. "How much did you put in his drink?"

"Twenty drops."

They buttoned their spencers as they stepped into the night air. "Twenty? It is a wonder he lasted that long."

"Once it became clear he knew nothing about the murder, I felt it was best to extricate ourselves from his clutches without the use of firearms . . ."

". . . or knives."

"Or knives."

The ladies' path turned towards the heart of Alderwood. "A prudent course of action," Penelope declared.

Walt withdrew her pipe from her pocket. After adding a bit of tobacco, she lit it in spite of the breeze. "Where to next then, miss?"

"As the night is fine and my aunt thinks I am abed with a headache, would you, perchance, be willing to involve yourself in a bit of subterfuge?"

"Of course." The mischievous glint of Walt's eye shone brighter than the waxing moon. "And if we have sufficient time, I wouldn't say no to a brawl as well."

Penelope chuckled. "If only we could be so fortunate."

# CHAPTER 17

## The Chapter with the Diary

"The potential of a psychometrist's gift is frequently underappreciated. Such gifts could revolutionise the legal system. Rather than relying upon conjecture, investigations could be led by concrete facts."

*Sir William Garrow PC KC FRS*

"The third floor!?"

"Yes."

Walt stopped at a door opening to the hall to stare out the window at the adjacent red-stone lodging house—James's house, to be precise. "Your plan is to cross the gap between this building and that building?"

Penelope selected two boards piled near the derelict stairs. "Precisely."

The moon shone through the missing window panes, illuminating the women's footprints on the grimy floor.

Walt clung to the bannister, trying each step. The dust of crumbling plaster swirled as her skirt swept the stairs. "This is a horrible plan."

Once they had gained the third floor of the abandoned building, Penelope pushed aside a door that clung to its frame by one hinge. The fire in her eyes could have lit a ballroom. "It is brilliant."

"Brilliantly horrible," Walt grumbled.

As the window's glass had fallen down into the alley below years ago, it did not need to be pried open. With Walt's aid, one board was slid across the three-foot gap to rest on the windowsill outside James's room. The deafening scrape of rough wood against brick drew the attention of a stray wyvern cuddling a fox terrier on a doorstep below. It huffed at the pair, the gentle glow of its flame sac visible in the inky shadows.

Walt leaned out the window, looking at the packed dirt earth below, twenty-four or so feet below, and then to the sky. The odour of rain hung in the air. Her feet shuffled back, putting distance between her and her early grave. "Are you certain he is out?"

With the steady hand of a proficient, Penelope rolled the hem of her skirt towards her waist, revealing a set of thin, knee-length trousers. Ribbons sewn across her natural waistline were paired and then tied to bustle her dress. Though she looked silly, it was practical, and preferable to falling to one's death.

"I am quite certain he has left for the evening and will not return for several hours." The second board joined the first. "Ready then?"

Walt began the task of bustling her own skirt, though with less care. "No."

"Be a good lass and steady the boards."

"Call me a lass again, and one of the boards might become dislodged. Pity."

As Penelope's knees rested on the windowsill, her heart most certainly did not race, and she did not sweat profusely. She would be fine. It was just twenty-nine inches across (and twenty-four feet down). Simple.

She glanced back at her friend, seeking support. Walt shrugged. "Try not to die. I haven't yet saved enough to purchase a cottage in the country where I can smoke my pipe and read books all day."

Though death stared her in the face as she rose to her feet, Penelope glanced back. "It is a good thing you are not a gentleman, or that line would have secured my undying love." A gust of wind whipped the fabric of her thin trousers.

Walt's hand shot out to steady her friend. "No thanks, miss. Though you're lovely, I prefer my own company."

In a display of agility uncommon for a lady (though not uncommon for one who spent her Mondays, Wednesdays, and Fridays balancing on logs, climbing trees, and hanging from branches), Penelope crossed the gap, opened the window, and slid inside. She turned and extended a hand to Walt. "See, simple."

Unlike her employer, Walt decided to crawl across the boards. Also, unlike Penelope, rather than gracefully alight from the window, she sort of rolled—feet flailing in the air—and fell onto the bed next to the window before tumbling to the floor, where she landed with a resounding thud. "Would have been awkward if he'd been home."

Penelope lit a candle to better survey the room. It was unchanged from her previous visit, though only one coat hung near the door. By the faint light of the candle, she observed that both baskets sat on the table. The cups of tea remained, unwashed, where she had left them.

"Should I look for the usual?" Walt had procured a candle of her own.

"Poisons, secret letters, diaries, and bribe money?" Penelope crossed the threadbare rug to the mantel to search for the card.

"Obviously."

A quick nod was acknowledgement enough for Walt to begin "perusing without permission." It was then that Penelope spotted the note from the second basket tucked amongst the odds and ends on the mantel. James, then, was a dowser. Its place on the mantel, surrounded by objects of interest, convinced her. Though unless he also possessed its kin gift, listening, also known as psychometry, he could only sense its importance, not its history.

She glanced over her shoulder to discover Walt on her hands and knees, sweeping a hand under the mattress. Her fingers fluttered as she turned towards the mantel once more.

It was a fine paper, a detail she had not noticed previously. Careful not to disturb the other trinkets, she lifted it and cradled it in her hands. Her eyes drifted closed.

Glimmers of its life in the forest and its transition into paper flashed through her mind like the flickering of a fire's light through closed eyes. The sharp pressure of a quill's tip digging into its surface caused her to wince. Eager to catch a glimpse of the writer, she relinquished her connection to her consciousness and delved into the vision of the past so deeply that she lost all sense of self.

The scratch of the quill blocked out all sound as the writer's face came into focus. When it did, Penelope gasped, snapping her back to the present. A chill rattled her teeth as she replaced the card.

"You all right?"

Penelope shook away the lingering sensations. She turned. Walt stood near the table. Even in the dim light of the candle, she could spot a few crumbs clinging to her lip. "Are you eating?"

Not distracted by the accusation disguised as a question, Walt considered her, curious. "I was hungry."

As a distraction was in order, Penelope dropped to her knees and swept her hand across the underside of the fireside chairs. "Have we not discussed before how unprofessional it is to eat while perusing the contents of a stranger's room?"

"You and your fancy words." Walt placed a balled hand upon her hips and bent forward at the waist. "It's snooping. *Snoo*-ping."

As neither of the wingbacks hid a secret compartment, Penelope checked the underside of the table and the mismatched chairs that belonged to it. Satisfied that the room had nothing else to disclose, she rose and dusted her hands against her trousers. "Well, I think there is nothing—"

The clearing of Walt's throat drew her eye. She stood across the table with a look more ascendant than Mary Fitzherbert's during her secret wedding to Prinny (also known as George, Prince of Wales) in 1785. In her hand, she held a journal.

Penelope ignored the smirk on her face and snatched it from her.

When she sat at the table, she was polite enough to wait for Walt to draw the other chair beside her before she opened the journal. It lay open, its spine long broken by frequent use.

*September 3rd, 1810*
*Today, I tripped on the rug in the hall again. I dropped the washing. Can you believe it? He stopped to help me collect it.*

*September 12th, 1810*
*In my chamber, I discovered this note*
*with a bouquet of wildflowers.*

Pressed between its pages, spotted by droplets of tea, lay the dried petals of yellow roses and a note. It read, *Roses for the prettiest flower in the world.*

Walt scoffed. Penelope palmed the note. And the page was turned.

*October 10th, 1810*
*Today, we stole into the wilderness behind the*
*manor. He packed the most scrumptious treats.*
*I think he may love me.*

*November 15th, 1810*
*While I dusted the west wing, he sneaked*
*up behind me and kissed my neck . . .*

*November 21st, 1810*
*He came to my room last night . . .*

After a cursory glance at the details (which were quite explicit), Penelope began to flip the page. Walt stayed her hand. "Hold on. I had not yet finished reading that one." Regardless, the page was turned.

The next few pages were filled with much of the same (much, much more, in fact); however, after the New Year, the entries took a turn.

*January 5th, 1811*
*He was peevish today. Personal affairs, he says.*

*January 21st, 1811*
*We had a row today . . .*

*February 8th, 1811*
*I found this note beneath my pillow. Should I go?*

A folded scrap of paper read, *Come to me this night, my love. Forgive and quite forget old faults.*
"Do you think she suspected he quoted Henry VI?"
Penelope turned towards her assistant, stunned.
She shrugged. "What? My ole dad played Henry VI once. I helped him practise his lines."

*February 26th, 1811*
*I have given my notice. To home I will go. I cannot go on without him.*

The pages beyond that date were blank.
Penelope closed the journal and pushed it aside. It slid, as if by magic, to the place in front of Walt, who tore it open. While her assistant flipped through the entries once

more, lingering on the naughty ones, Penelope turned aside, her fingers dancing across the note she had secreted in her pocket. As she closed her eyes, a fleeting vision of Grace, eyes alight as she read the note, rose before her. She pressed deeper into the vision—

The smack of the front door against the hall rang with such force that the entire house quaked, causing Walt to drop the apple she had stolen. Penelope started.

{Narrator's Official Complaint to the Author: Characters must stop interrupting my exposition. How am I ever going to divulge the author of the note and our sleuth's suspicions as to the identity of Grace's lover if characters continue to storm into a chapter before I have neatly—}

Slurred words mingled with shouts announced the arrival of a tenant who, by the volume and incoherence of his speech, had swallowed a hare (in other words, was tipsy). Neither Walt nor Penelope breathed as they heard, "Mr Sullivan, if you . . ."

With the tips of her fingers, Penelope snuffed the candles out. As James still had both his eyes, he could not have read his sister's journal; therefore, Penelope felt no guilt in stuffing it down the front of her dress before she seized Walt's hand and yanked her towards the bed.

"Bit forward—"

"Do not flatter yourself."

The clomp of a heavy tread grew louder, indicating that James was on the move and approaching the second-storey landing.

Penelope shoved her assistant under James's bed before she dived under it as well.

Tucking her legs against her chest, she hoped that the combination of darkness and drink would render her invisible to his eyes. "Walt, I must know; why the spoons?"

"Well, miss, when polished, they become tiny mirrors. Obviously."

Penelope scarcely had time to scoff at Walt's insincere reply before the door smacked open. By the light of the moon, they observed James stumble across the room towards the—

An "Oof!" escaped their lips as every pound of what could be described as a strapping young man came crashing down upon the mattress, and, by virtue of the bed being low to the floor, upon them.

Whilst she wondered whether her jar of bruise remover contained a sufficient amount to treat the day's injuries, the inebriated fellow either died or slipped off into a noiseless slumber.

A few minutes of silence sufficed to reassure the trespassers that it was safe to emerge. Silently, they wiggled free from their hiding spots. After returning the candles and chair to their original places, they tiptoed across the room, through the door, and into the night.

# CHAPTER 18
## The Chapter with Toast

"A rolling stone may gather no moss, but a forest
dragon will."

*Ben Scott — Whisperer*

Eager to mull over the intelligence afforded by her perusal
of the contents of James's room, Penelope bade farewell to
Walt, leaving her comfortably curled in her chair with the
evening paper.

More concerned about predators who wandered on
two feet rather than four, she selected the path that would
lead her through a grove of elder trees. Her pistol was at
the ready, as was a satchel of sugared berries.

Her feet padded along a narrow path, one that cut
through the ancient woodland. Time passed elsewhere,
but not here. Beneath these boughs shrouded in moss and
draped with vines, wild creatures could seek refuge from
the encroachment of cities. This forest drew them lovingly
into her heart, shielding them from the harsh world of men.

In the stillness, Penelope could think at last. Grace had
a lover; that much was certain. From the journal, she had
gleaned the following:

1. *Her beau was a he.*
2. *Poor Grace was besotted enough to risk both her reputation and her position.*
3. *Their affair had not been all rainbows and fairy dust.*
4. *She had left to either follow him or flee from him.*

A breeze coursed through the treetops, sweeping through the forest like a wave. She paused. It drew the tension from her heart as a poultice would wick away an infection. After several minutes, she pressed on; the rustle of brush and the calls of owls had soothed her.

In her vision of the note from the basket, Penelope had seen neither lord nor lady. It had been the Pilkingtons' housekeeper, Mrs Bates, a formidable woman known for her adroit management of a household of ninnies. Of course, the fact that she had written the note did not solidify her as a suspect, but rather, insinuated that a member of the family had been involved in . . .

A heat crept across her skin, raising the hairs on her arms. Penelope froze. Her hand did not withdraw her pistol. Whatever lurked in the wood that night could not be harmed by bullets. She could sense it, the magic, the palpable power coursing through the roots and vines, hushing the wind.

Unlike charms, this power smelled not of flowers nor wet earth but of the forest—a cacophony of scents so intoxicating she could hardly breathe. With care, she turned, her senses reaching outward like hands groping in the shadow.

Then . . . she felt it behind her. She waited, knowing she was powerless to protect herself. However, it did not attack her or disappear into the darkness. No, dear Reader, it nudged her.

With due deference, she bowed her head and turned with care to face a dragon. This, however, was no house pet or stone dragon—creatures which, though lovely, had sacrificed their power for comfort. This was a forest dragon, a keeper of the wild.

"An honour, Sir Dragon." She curtseyed low. Her eyes met his—pine-green starbursts bordered by brown edges. He appraised her, a pixie clad in muslin with feathers in her bonnet, sensing her gifts, no doubt, but also her intentions.

A moment passed before he bowed, the sign that he meant her no harm. Then, quite unexpectedly, his lips spread into a toothy grin.

"My name is Penelope Sedgewick, and you are . . . ?"

On cue, he picked up a stick with his mouth and began to draw in the earth. Though she did not expect him to share his true name—one that could not be spoken, only felt—she suspected he had adopted an English name to use when interacting with humans. Perhaps he had named himself Aspen, Deluge, or Fury?

As he eagerly sketched, she observed him. Like others of his kind, he was roughly the size of a horse. After all, if he were the size of an earth dragon, for instance, he would not be able to weave along narrow game trails or make his nest among the treetops.

Unlike others of his kind, he had suffered. Where should have sprouted a beard of moss and flowers was bare, leathery skin, shorn clean. His horns, though intact, had been sanded and polished, then mutilated with carvings. And as he finished his drawing, she noted that he favoured his hind leg.

Her aunt had been right: she need not fear the creatures that dwelt in the wood, for true monsters had not scales or fur but wore coats and carried parasols. Penelope swallowed the acrid taste of loathing.

Her dragon friend, or so she hoped, had cast aside his stick and looked at her expectantly. In the earth, she noted a well-drawn slice of bread. She turned to him. "Would you have me call you Bread?"

His look communicated, *Are you serious? No, you cannot be serious. Try again.*

"I apologise. I have never been good at guessing games." She stepped nearer. "I would guess Slice, but that feels equally silly."

He took up the stick again and added swirls to the drawing that resembled—

"Toast! Is your name Toast?" Penelope shouted excitedly.

Toast wiggled with delight, the tip of his tail swishing side to side.

"It is a pleasure to make your acquaintance, Sir Toast." She curtseyed low.

Toast pranced (as best he could) around her, displaying his deep green and honey-yellow colouring. He fanned his wings skyward. Her eye traced the root-like pattern of his vessels and ligaments as the light of the moon shone through them.

"You are quite the specimen. Very handsome."

He waggled his eyebrows to communicate, *Do you think I do not know I am handsome? Hmm?*

She giggled. "And a bit mischievous, I would hazard."

He pursed his lips. *As are you, no doubt. A lady wandering after dark in the forest. Scandalous.*

"I know." Penelope shrugged.

Besides the injury he had suffered, it was clear even to her untrained eye that Toast was a trifle thin. From her pocket, she withdrew a satchel containing sugar-coated berries. She emptied its contents into her hand, which she then extended to her newfound friend. "It is all my pockets will carry, but perhaps you will accept these as a token of my esteem."

He nodded his head, then gently, taking care not to eat any fingers, licked the treat from her palm, swallowing the berries in one gulp. Penelope had never known hunger, yet she was aware that a few berries would do nothing to satiate his empty stomach.

"Toast, may I inquire as to what brings you to this corner of the forest?" She scratched the skin just under his chin. "It is well known that an ancient she-dragon they call Hallstrom cares for this region of the wood. So how did you come across these paths?"

Dear Toast ducked his head.

"I do not mean to intrude." She crouched low and peered into his eye. Her throat tightened. There, behind the power, behind the millennia of wisdom, lay pain. "If I can be of service, please . . ."

A thought lifted the corner of his mouth into a crooked grin. He hopped back to his stick to take it up again. After his tail erased his name, he began to outline the shape of a man, yet not a normal man.

"Is that a Sasquatch?" she wondered incredulously.

He nodded with such eagerness that his entire body bobbed.

"The Grey Man?"

He nodded again.

"Am I to understand that you are seeking the Yeti?"

Toast pursed his lips. *Yeeesss. I had thought you were clever. Was I wrong?*

Slighted but not too offended, Penelope placed her hands on her hips. "Of course I am clever; I just had not known the Yeti travelled this far south and, for what it matters, that he actually existed."

"Of course I exist."

In a blink, Penelope drew her pistol and pointed it in the direction of the bass voice while Toast leapt in front of her, coiling his tail protectively around her.

"Please, do not shoot. I have not brought my sewing kit and have only just recovered from my last encounter with a bullet."

# CHAPTER 19

## The Chapter with Ben, the Yeti

"A yeti, Ben Scott of Ben Macdui, Scotland, formally disputes Parliament's findings regarding his existence. According to Mr Scott, he does, in fact, exist; however, as Parliament has decreed that he does not, his application to reinstate his existence has been denied."

*Minutes from His Majesty's Most Honourable Privy Council, 1809*

Penelope, as a rational being, had never given the existence of yetis much thought—that was, until one stood before her with the moon at his back, silhouetting his massive frame.

"It would appear that you have no intention of shooting me. Please, kindly lower your weapon."

With caution, she pocketed her pistol, though her finger remained on the trigger. Her other hand rested on Toast's tail, which remained protectively wrapped around her. "And who are you, sir, coming upon a gentlewoman and her dragon acquaintance unannounced?"

He raised his hands skyward and turned until the moon lit his face. He was, in fact, a yeti. Though more man than ape, he towered above Penelope. Locks of auburn hair with streaks of blond covered him from head to toe, or so she presumed. Unlike the unflattering drawings she had seen printed in publications and journals, this yeti wore breeches, a shirt, and a linen waistcoat with a fob watch.

"My name is Mr Scott, or Ben to my friends. A pleasure to make your acquaintance, Miss . . ."

She straightened. "Miss Sedgewick. How do you do?"

"Ahhh, Miss Sedgewick of Birch Hallow." A knowing look dawned in his eye. He bowed. Penelope noted the hint of his Scottish origins seeping into the cadence of his speech. "I heard the Beast of Bodmin Moor visited your estate last spring, or will it be next spring? I forget."

Toast flashed her a wry grin—the yeti was a seer, no doubt. Seers were notorious for inhabiting a world where the lines between past and future were blurry at best. Strange. Though most were guarded, careful not to reveal their gift to strangers, he had essentially confessed his not two minutes into their acquaintance. Then again, the man who stood before them with bright, sapphire eyes was covered in hair. Being a seer was not the strangest thing about him by far.

"And you are . . ." He held out his hand, palm turned upward. Toast stepped forward. "Ah, Toast. A pleasure to make your acquaintance. And am I to understand you have been seeking me?"

Toast bobbed his head. So, Mr Scott was a seer *and* a whisperer—an unusual combination. Nurturers and whispers were a kinship pairing, as were dowsers and psychometrists (or sniffers, as they were often called). True seers were rare; those blessed, or cursed, with a second gift were rarer still.

The night air nipped at Penelope's cheeks. She flipped up the collar of her cerulean spencer to block out the wind. Her chattering teeth drew the attention of both the man and the dragon.

Toast frowned. Before she could object, he closed his eyes. She sensed a wave of energy pulsing outward through her chest and into the night. The air stilled.

"Toast, none of that." Mr Scott wagged his finger. Penelope noted that the calloused palms of his hands were those of a man. "These are Hallstrom's woods, and she won't take kindly to you if you carry on like that."

Though the dragon shrugged, Penelope hazarded that he would not welcome an encounter with a miffed she-dragon named Hallstrom. Who would?

The yeti waved the pair to a fallen log where Penelope might sit. He gathered sticks and fallen branches, arranging them to form a fire. From the satchel that hung at his hip, he withdrew a canister of matches.

"Tell me, Toast. What brings you to our corner of the world?" He struck the match. It blazed to life, lighting his face—a kind one, Penelope thought.

"Mm-hmm." He nodded. Without regard for his breeches' integrity, he knelt on the earth. His other hand cupped the tender flame as he lowered it towards the kindling. The dry moss and wispy twigs caught. Distracted, he murmured, "Yes, I see."

Penelope rolled her eyes. It was for this very reason that whisperers were considered odd, even by other Folk.

Though *they* could communicate with all manner of beasts, the rest of society could not.

She tried to brush off the offence. After all, this poor man was a legend, a tale of lore told to convince children to mind their manners lest he eat them for supper. He did not have opportunities to mingle in society often, much less practise polite conversation.

Toast trotted towards her and turned twice before he settled at Penelope's side. His tail curled round her back to block the chill. He stole a peek at her over his shoulder, smirking.

"No, we are not being rude." Mr Scott glanced from the dragon to the lady and back again. "Are we?"

"*You* are." Penelope straightened her shoulders. "However, if your manners improve and you help my friend, I shall endeavour to forgive you."

Mr Scott bowed. "Thank you, kind lady."

With a hand the size of a dinner plate, he fanned the flame, coaxing it to burn brighter. Penelope angled her face towards it, basking in its heat.

"Toast was informing me of his journeys." Another log was added to the fire. "He escaped his former owner not three weeks ago. A badger told him to seek me here to receive treatment for his injured leg and some advice."

Swearing to pursue the matter of his former owner another day, Penelope stroked the ridge of Toast's back. "Advice regarding?"

He rose, retrieved his bag, and knelt beside Toast's injured foot. "A home."

Penelope's eyebrows knitted together. She observed the forest dragon. To describe the look on his face as pained and leave it at that would be an insult. Beyond his starburst eyes, deep in the recesses, lurked grief so raw Penelope stifled a gasp when she caught a glimpse of it.

Mr Scott sat on the fallen tree across from her, resting his elbows on his knees so as to be able to look into Toast's eyes. "May I?"

The dragon dipped his chin in reply.

From his bag, Mr Scott withdrew a leather roll-up bag. It was worn and aged, with shells, scales, and feathers adorning the tie. "Tokens of appreciation," he explained.

A bed of last year's leaves formed a cushion upon which he sat next to Toast's injured leg. He unfastened the knot and laid the bag flat. Rare herbs, oils, healer's tinctures, and sprigs were nestled in pockets, along with a few instruments. From his pocket, he tugged a miniature magnifying glass free. Gently, he lifted his patient's paw to begin his examination. "Forest dragons, as you may know, are among a family of ward dragons. Legends say—"

Toast scoffed to communicate, *They are not legends; they are memories. Just because humans cannot pass on their histories through thought does not mean we cannot.*

"I apologise." Mr Scott reached up and scratched his chin. He unbuttoned and rolled up the sleeves of his pressed shirt. A lock of chestnut hair peeked through the gaps between the buttons at his chest. "The memories passed down from their history tell us that their eggs sprang from the earth beside the first trees. They were created to protect the woodlands and forests. The lifeforce of the forest is the source of their power."

Penelope stood so that she could wrap her arms around Toast's neck. He sank his chest into her, nuzzling her as she stroked his head.

Each forest dragon's horns were unique, though they generally resembled those of a stag. As she held him, she observed the swirling patterns and roses that had been carved into his. Though the infant buds of spring flowers peeked through the honey-coloured scales on the back of his neck, his mane of wildflowers and vines had been violently stripped. The monsters.

After applying a compress of leaves, Mr Scott retrieved a spotless strip of fabric. "When a forest dragon is removed from their home, one of two things occurs: either the forest fades and dies . . ."

A shiver coursed through Toast's body straight into Penelope's heart.

". . . or another dragon can claim it as its own." He secured the compress to the paw. "Toast tells me that he was taken from his home some time ago. When he escaped, he returned home, only to discover it had been claimed by another."

Mr Scott rose to add a log as wide as a woman's waist to the fire. "Though Toast could have challenged him, forest dragons are not the warring sort, and besides . . ." He stoked the embers. ". . . the other dragon had kept his home from fading; he had nurtured it well. He could not take the life of one who had cared for his forest in his absence."

Penelope's eyes stung—from the smoke, of course. "And where will he go now?"

"That is precisely why he has come. He had hoped I might have heard of a forest in need of tending."

"And have you?" She held her breath.

"No." He shook his head. His hand stroked his beard. "I have not."

She twirled a sable lock that had broken free at the nape of her neck. "What will happen if he does not find a home?"

"Either he will wander, or . . ." His voice caught in his throat. Turning, he squatted beside the fire. ". . . he will fade."

Toast nudged his friend with the tip of his snout as though to say, *It will work itself out,* before resting his head on the earth and shielding his eyes with his paws.

Her face appeared serene, but the yeti's words ignited a flame inside Penelope. As the fire that had been started with sticks and matches burned bright, warming her extended palms, the blaze ignited by the dragon's story threatened to consume her. The gold in her hazel eyes shone, reflecting the determination within.

"No." Her voice did not tremor, nor did she shout. She spoke as though she could make it so simply by speaking the words. "That will not be."

Toast lifted his head to appraise her.

Penelope took his face in her hands, cradling it. "My estate will be your home. It has a small wilderness not under the care of a dragon, and plenty of land to expand it into a proper, albeit humble, home."

*I cannot ask this of you* was indicated in the shake of his head.

She held his gaze. Hope shone in his eyes. "What use have I for acres upon acres of gardens and fields?"

Mr Scott continued to stoke the flames, unwilling, it would appear, to intrude.

"So long as you promise to leave a couple of acres to my aunt and to tolerate the zilant and the faedragon that live on our estate . . ."

Toast's lip turned upward into a sneer.

"None of that. They are quite tolerable." She scratched under his chin. "And as long as you permit my uncle to conduct his experiments in your wood; then I cannot think of an impediment. Have we a deal?" Penelope extended her hand.

For a moment, Toast appraised her, no doubt wondering whether this fae-like woman in a lace could be trusted. Clearly, she passed muster, for he pressed his nose into her hand.

Though her eyes could not perceive it, Penelope felt a golden cord extend from the dragon's heart to knot itself to hers, binding them to one another. A vision of the world Toast knew flitted through her mind, its life coursing through every branch, every leaf, every vine. She could hear a mother rabbit in her burrows comforting her kittens. The barn owl, who had flown far from home, complained of an empty stomach and hoped a mouse would wander into the open. Even the birch trees towering overhead had thoughts, though they were less clear, more primal. Too soon, the world faded to the dullness she had always known, and all that remained were the sincere eyes of her friend.

She dropped her hand and gathered her reticule. "Shall we depart?"

"Not 'til dawn." Mr Scott had settled against the other log. She had not noticed, but he wore sturdy boots, the sort worn by farmers. "There are dark things moving in the woods tonight."

Penelope was tempted to chuckle until she remembered that before her sat a seer. She glanced at

Toast, who had already begun to settle in for the night. Since the staff at Birch Hallow had strict instructions not to disturb her between the hours of nine at night and eight the following morning, she shrugged. A nap would suit her well, she supposed.

With a flick of his tail, Toast invited her to curl against him. Thankfully, she had been sensible enough to wear a dress as dark as midnight for this evening's escapades; the black earth would leave no stains for her maid to discover tomorrow.

As she nodded off to sleep, she wondered at the notion that a simple elopement had evolved into a murder investigation involving at least one of the leading families in the county.

# CHAPTER 20

## The Chapter with the Clean Stockings

"I am happy to find that gentlemen, men of
honour, and even military men in some cases,
appeal to the civil laws of their country, when
challenged, instead of the sword; and they appear
to be countenanced in so doing."

*Trusler, Rev Dr John, and Chesterfield, Lord, Principles of
Politeness and of knowing the world*

Dragon pillows are not comfortable, or so Penelope
decided when she awoke. It was the songbirds who
disturbed her slumber. For, despite the early hour, they
had schedules to keep, which they discussed in melodies
composed of bright chirps and tweets.

Ugh! Penelope abhorred cheeriness before sunrise. It
ought to have been an offence punishable by . . .

A prodding by what she hazarded was a dragon's
tail roused her. Her eyes fluttered open to behold Toast's
toothy grin in all its splendour. She scowled.

"If we are to be friends, you must never wake me
before dawn again."

Her scaly friend lowered his head.

Had she not had a murder to solve and an assistant to keep in pipe tobacco, she would have sent herself to the gallows for eliciting that look. "I am sorry. Perhaps, for you, I shall make an exception."

In acknowledgement, he nuzzled her cheek.

Mr Scott's place across the fire was empty, signalling that they were safe to venture forth. She bent to tie her sensible leather boots. "Would you like to see your new home at sunrise?"

Toast nodded his head with such enthusiasm that the tip of his tail bobbed.

"Shall we?" she asked.

The forest dragon bowed low, sweeping his wing towards the path.

Her nose crinkled as she chuckled. "Quite the gentleman."

Together they strolled in the forest. As the sun had not yet peeked above the horizon, they were in no rush. Though not one to wax poetic, Penelope described the finer points of Birch Hallow and the kindness of its inhabitants as best she could. Toast listened, dipping his chin periodically.

"We shall tell them we encountered one another on my morning walk."

He gave her a sidelong glance, which she understood to mean, _We_ _shall not tell them anything._ _You_ _can tell them whatever you like._

A droplet of water plopped on the tip of her nose. Penelope gazed skyward. A second landed in her eye. She cursed before brushing it away.

Before a third could land on her, she felt something whoosh past. Toast, her knight in scaly armour, had extended his wing over her head to serve as an umbrella.

"Charmer."

He shrugged.

The hazy glow of the morning sun trickled over the horizon as they emerged from the forest. They had only to pass through a field that divided her estate from Mrs Stevenson's home. Though she abhorred sunrises on principle, she could not deny the unrushed beauty of creation breathlessly waiting for dawn.

Caught up in the wonder of it all, she observed the waves of wind coursing through the trees, the man crumpled in the field, the birds calling to one another in . . .

Blast! Penelope exhaled audibly. Nothing like a second corpse to ruin a morning stroll. Taking her skirts in one hand, she sprinted across a knoll towards the body. Toast followed close, his eyes sweeping the field for danger.

She motioned for him to stay back as she approached the body. If he was dead, then she must try to preserve the scene. And if he still clung to life, seeing a dragon hovering over him could be the final straw.

"Alert me if anyone approaches."

The dragon stood tall, squinting into the distance.

Though a stone's throw still separated them, she recognised the man. There, splayed across the wet earth, lay Mr Montagu, dead.

{Narrator's Note: As we have happened upon *another* murder and as our heroine is a stickler for detail, now would be a good time to insert a

147

bookmark. (Do NOT dog-ear the page. I repeat, DO NOT.) Refill your tea, complete the chore you have been putting off, etc. Of course, I am teasing. Let us continue.}

Her gaze swept across her path, careful to examine each knot of grass and clump of wildflowers. A chill radiated from the rain-soaked field, though it did not trouble her; her entire being was engrossed in observing the scene.

Even at a distance of a few strides, it was evident he was beyond hope. There was an unnatural stillness known only in death. Penelope might have been no seer, nor healer, but as a sniffer, she could sense the hint of power tied to each living soul. Mr Montagu—handsome, raven-haired, Mr Montagu—was nothing but a shell.

"He is dead," she called to Toast. The lift of his shoulders suggested that he had known already.

Though averse to squatting, she lowered herself into the unladylike pose so as to spare the embroidered lilies on the hem of her dress. She touched the back of Mr Montagu's hand. A hint of warmth lingered still, but it would vanish within the hour.

The innumerable capes of his greatcoat indicated he was dressed for travel. He wore boots and black breeches, both intended for crossing fields rather than sipping tea in drawing rooms. Though the rain had ceased less than a quarter of an hour prior, the shoulders of his coat were damp, not soaked as she would expect had he been out of doors for even half an hour. Peculiar.

As his coat was black, she did not immediately notice the wound to his chest. There, just above his heart, was

148

a bullet wound. Crimson blood stained his crisp, white cravat. No other injuries, fatal or otherwise, presented themselves.

"Toast," she called. "Do be a dear and help me roll the body onto its side."

Though he still limped, it was less pronounced. In the morning's filtered light, his colouring reminded her of midday sunlight shining through a canopy of beech trees.

"You are not squeamish, are you?"

He pressed his lips into a flat line in reply.

"Obviously not." Penelope shifted towards Mr Montagu's feet. "Careful. I want to check for an exit wound."

A second wound lay just below his last right rib. A physician could decide definitively whether Mr Montagu's killer had stood at a high angle or whether the bullet had bounced about a bit before exiting. Though blood soaked the earth beneath him, she would not hazard a guess as to how much.

Before Toast returned him to his original position, she noted that the back of his jacket and the hair on the back of his head were drenched with dew. His hat lay an arm's length away.

"Thank you." She patted his side. "Have you any observations to make?"

He poked his leathery chin at the weapon lying near Mr Montagu's feet. It was a fine double-barrel flintlock whose worn handle suggested it had been used often.

"Yes, the hour and the presence of a weapon would suggest a duel, and yet . . ." She shuffled to his feet and sighed. "As I suspected. He did not die in this spot, or even out of doors, I would wager."

To get a closer look, Toast craned his neck and studied Mr Montagu's stockings. The arch of his brow conveyed, *Unless you are a seer, I do not know how you can deduce where he was killed.*

Penelope suppressed a grin. Oh, how she loved occasionally showing off. "See here." she directed her friend to observe his stockings. "Stockings that have crossed a field to arrive at this location are never this clean."

Toast nodded, impressed.

"And here. The bottoms of his shoes are scuffed but not dirty, as though he had been indoors for hours. Even if he had ridden here, I would expect to find mud, bits of grass or leaves."

She rose and circled the body once. "It is precisely like Grace."

The forest dragon pursed his lips and tilted his head to one side.

"Oh, yes. I have not told you about her." Her eyes roved the ground, searching for additional clues. "In summary, she was a maid we discovered dead. It has been deemed an accident, but a missing sugar bowl has convinced me that the scene was staged."

*You certainly do happen upon a great number of murders*, was conveyed by a lifted brow.

"Only of late." She shivered. From the cold, of course, not from the complex and quite unsettling punchbowl feelings of elation mixed with anxiety and garnished with dread. "Both deaths have been arranged to appear like one thing when, in fact, they were another."

Penelope stood over the gun, wondering what it could betray. Her fingers itched. She glanced at Toast, who had

150

turned his attention to the male common blue butterfly with periwinkle wings that had landed on the tip of his snout.

Though the identification of fingerprints as a science was in its infancy at best, she thought it wise not to handle the weapon. Instead, she placed her knuckle on its muzzle and closed her eyes.

Flashes of targets rushed past until a man stood directly in front of her. Penelope willed the memory to slow. A clear sky, rather than the overcast one of that day, encircled a field, one that felt familiar but that she could not place. Opposite her stood a man dressed plainly. Unlike the vision of the housekeeper who had written the card, this man's face shone clear—Mr Andrews, a farmer, a respectable one if her memory served her right. Anger contorted his face.

As she expected, the men marked their paces, turned, and—

The convulsion of the pistol's recoil knocked her back into reality and onto the drenched earth. Into the canvas of grey, murky clouds overhead popped Toast's concerned face.

She sprang to her feet. "I am fine."

*If you say so.* He examined her.

Not wishing to linger and risk being discovered at the scene of a(nother) murder, she collected her reticule. "Shall we?"

Toast looked at her, then the body. *And what of him?*

"Not to worry. I shall quietly notify the magistrate."

As they walked away, Penelope did not steal a final look at the field. And, most definitely, she did not thank the heavens that this murder was not hers to solve . . . probably.

# CHAPTER 21

## The Chapter with All the Forgetfulness

"'I should like balls infinitely better,' she replied,
'if they were carried on in a different manner; but
there is something insufferably tedious in the usual
process of such a meeting. It would surely be much
more rational if conversation instead of dancing
were made the order of the day.'"

*Untitled Work in Progress by A Lady*

Although Penelope had awoken before dawn, she was not
the first to arrive at the library that morning. Seated in his
usual chair was Uncle Archie, with Cerberus to his right,
napping.

"Good morning," she signed. Before helping herself to
a plate of breads and fruits, she circled the polished table
and planted a kiss on her uncle's forehead. His wizened
hair tickled her nose. She noted that he looked especially
rumpled that morning, as though he had dressed without
the aid of his valet.

"'Morning, my dear." He broke off a corner of honey
bread and placed it on the hand-painted plate with gold

accents that had been set before his faedragon. Drowsily, she lifted her head, sniffed, and, as the treat appeared enticing, gulped down the bread.

There were the usual papers and books stacked about his chair. "I hear Birch Hallow has become the home of a forest dragon."

She nodded her dark head. Her locks were gathered into a timeless knot, as usual. "Yes. His name is Toast."

"Toast? Are you sure you understood him? Not Hellfire or Drakonis? Even a Fitzwilliam?"

"Yes, I am certain." She stirred her tea so vigorously that it became a teacup-sized whirlpool. "He was seeking a home when I happened upon him this morning. As we have proven to be poor gardeners, with the west field in disrepair and the wood a swamp, I thought we should entrust them to his care."

Uncle Archie tipped his chin. "Cerberus and I shall wander down later today to welcome him properly."

The hum of silence filled the space, absent of the utterances and patting sounds that accompany signed language, interrupted only by the rustling of the newspaper or the wind rattling the windows. Penelope read *The Alderwood Courier*, a rag so overrun by conjecture, gossip, and adverts that one writer was sufficient to contribute the few newsworthy articles it contained.

She scanned the pages. There had been a yeti sighting near Sable's house. A report of a tradesman found bloodied and beaten on the main thoroughfare drew her eye. No name had been included, but a crude sketch meant to stoke the reader's abhorrence of vices such as drink, gambling, and prostitution filled an eighth of the page. Penelope chuckled at the article's proximity to an advert for punch recipes and another for prayer services.

When Uncle Archie made a noise in his throat, indicating he disagreed with a line in the letter he was perusing, likely from Lord Alderwood, she laid aside her paper and studied him. The image of the young man mocking her uncle rose in her mind. Her throat grew tight. No wonder her uncle created a world for himself where he would be valued by those wise enough to appreciate him.

When she contemplated how she had disappointed him, she would not have blamed Cerberus if she had lived up to her name and consume Penelope whole.

She tapped the table, causing the tea to slosh in her uncle's cup. He looked up, bushy eyebrows raised expectantly.

"Uncle," she signed. "I must apologise for neglecting to deliver your letter yesterday. If you will entrust it to me once more, I shall not fail you again."

His sun-spotted hand reached across the pile of books and journals to clasp hers. "Of course." He kissed her fingers, releasing the knot in her throat. "I have delivered this week's myself, but shall call upon my faithful Hermes in lilac with all of my future missives."

The precise tread of her aunt echoed in the hall. Penelope signalled her approach.

Uncle Archie gave her a knowing wink. "Incoming. Man the cannons."

Despite her best efforts, a giggle erupted from her just as the door to the drawing room opened to reveal Aunt Josephine. She wore black as usual, but since she had errands and calls to make, she had dressed in a particularly fine gown that complemented her dark hair and shockingly blue eyes. Penelope had never feared her aunt, but seeing her enter the room that morning with the confidence of Athena, she understood why lesser mortals might.

"Good morning, dear." Aunt Josephine squeezed her niece's shoulder as she passed to the sideboard. "Did you sleep well?"

Penelope had once stolen a chocolate from her aunt's dressing table. When she had been discovered a quarter of an hour later with the evidence still smudged on the cuffs of her dress, she had made a promise never to lie to her aunt again. And while not disclosing the precise nature of her gifts *could* be considered as lying by some, she had filed it under "omissions" instead. Which was why she felt horrible answering, "Yes, aunt, quite well."

Her aunt served herself breakfast, unsatisfied with her response.

"Though, now that you mention it, my pillow was . . ." *a dragon and my bed the forest floor* ". . . a tad lumpy. I think I shall have it replaced."

Content with her untruth, Aunt Josephine turned to her brother. "And you, why were you traipsing about the field this morning at dawn?"

The tea dribbling down her chin prevented Penelope from noticing her uncle fumble with his cup. Aunt Josephine handed her niece a handkerchief.

The redness creeping up her uncle's neck like an invasive weed convinced Penelope of two things: one, that he *had* ventured forth that morning, and two, that he was desperate to prevent his sister from asking more questions.

Feigning that she had misheard the question, she replied, "Yes, aunt, I was out this morning. I fancied an early walk. Have you heard? We have entrusted the care of our grounds to a forest dragon."

A pair of pursed lips was answer enough. "Yes." She topped up her brother's cup, neglecting Penelope's entirely. "Ambrose rushed out to meet him this morning and has not returned. If he is eaten——"

"Our new arrival would do no such thing."

Aunt Josephine ignored her niece's rudeness, though never had a slice of honey cake been so beaten and battered by a jam knife before. "Regardless, the gardener was quite put out."

"Of course. Could you remind him that he will still care for the gardens near the house? It is the wood and the fields, as well as the back lawn, that I have entrusted to Toast."

The corner of her aunt's mouth angled upward. "Toast, you say?"

"Yes, Aunt." She refilled her own teacup. To elicit sympathy and win over her aunt to Toast's cause, she dropped her voice. "He had been captured, removed from his forest, and turned into a spectacle."

Uncle Archie laid aside his journal. Even Cerberus raised her coral head to listen.

"They stripped him of his moss and they carved designs into his horns."

What passed through those three extraordinary minds that morning cannot be known, but it is safe to presume that they each contemplated several discreet means of dispatching and then disposing of Toast's former enslaver.

{Narrator's Note: An appalling rumour has circulated concerning a set of diagrams depicting a wall toppling onto a man (or woman) and a couple of complex recipes for untraceable poisons. Whether such items were discovered by the maid who tidied up that afternoon is neither here nor there. Half the manors in England contain death threats or poison recipes. Nothing to see here.}

"In that case," Uncle Archie signed, his eyes glassy, "he is welcome. Our home is his home now." He speared a berry with his fork. "After all, we loons must stick together."

Aunt Josephine raised her teacup in agreement. "As to unity, I presume that the pair of you will be in attendance for the ball this evening."

The niece and uncle looked at one another and then at her.

"The ball."

They shook their heads.

"*The* Pilkingtons' annual ball. The one I have on the schedule hung near the umbrellas."

Her uncle's round eyes indicated that he, too, had neglected to check the calendar that had been posted after the last ball they had forgotten.

"I see." As a genius in her own right, her aunt knew how best to effect change in her brother and niece. She did not storm nor rage nor lecture; no, her aunt deployed a more lethal weapon—guilt.

The three sat in silence, all perfectly aware of Aunt Josephine's intentions and still feeling horrible.

Uncle Archie signed first, "I apologise, sister. Of course we shall attend."

"As do I, Aunt. I shall be ready at eight."

With that, everyone resumed sipping their tea and dreading an evening of dancing, awkward stares, and mortifying silences.

# CHAPTER 22

## The Chapter with the Walking

"Though the creation of tinctures and talismans
colloquially known as "truth tellers" could benefit
the interrogation of suspects, they were universally
banned in 1798 when a batch was slipped into the
Prince Regent's tea. The secrets spilt that day nearly
led to the downfall of the empire."

*Magic: Spirit or Science, Page 87*

Penelope stood, mouth agape, eyes the size of saucers, in
the middle of her offices. "It is before noon."

"Yes," replied Walt, her feet draped over the arm of
her chair as usual.

"And you are awake."

Her assistant exhaled a perfect circle of smoke.
"Obviously."

"I . . ." Glued to the spot, Penelope stood with eyes
unfocused as she made sense of the situation. "In the last
forty-eight hours, I have been flirted with by a delectable
footman, discovered two murders, been chased by a pack
of drakes, met a yeti, befriended a dragon, and yet *this* is
the one revelation I can genuinely classify as shocking."

159

"I found the flirting was shocking . . ." Walt loped across the rug to the fireplace and tapped her ashes into the cold hearth. ". . . and hilarious."

Having finally recovered her senses, Penelope collected the stack of letters from her Limoges plate and sat at the uncluttered desk near the window to peruse them. "So the dead body was not surprising in the least? Hmm?"

"What can I say? Outside our little tête-à-têtes, I live a full life." Walt resumed her seat and downed a cup of tea as if it were a shot of cheap whiskey. "Just last week, I met a man with six fingers. Besides, yesterday at noon is not early."

"Am I to understand you have not slept in twenty-three hours?" Penelope's hands rhythmically broke each seal and unfolded the letters, stacking them neatly in a pile. She glanced up. With the filtered light of the window shining on her assistant's face, she could trace the signs of fatigue. Though Walt had changed into a dress the colour of wheat with a brown satin ribbon and completed her toilette, her caramel eyes were not as alert as usual.

Walt shrugged. "I had to finish investigating my ole brother Franny."

"Or your dear brother John." Penelope paused, glimpsing at the contents of the first letter. "And what have you discovered?

"Nothin'. Not a sighting, not a rumour, not so much as a whiff of a lone captain in the area."

"Are you certain?" She read the second letter, then the third; a suppressed grin flitted behind the composed mask she wore.

If eye-rolls made a noise, the one Walt shot at her employer would have been loud enough to wake the recently deceased Mr Montagu from his grave. "What do you take me for? I ain't no novice, miss. Kindly keep your doubts to yourself."

With the final letter having been read, Penelope rose, pushed the chair in, and slid her sage-green satin reticule (which complemented her gown nicely) onto her wrist. "It is as I thought."

As Penelope headed towards the door, Walt stood and hurried after her, though she did close and lock the door on her way out. "What is?"

"Precisely," Penelope called back, taking the stairs two at a time.

It was in the alley behind Cecilia's Cabinet that Walt caught up. "Precisely? You do realise you aren't making a lick of sense, don't you?"

"It all begins with Grace."

"No, Rose."

"No." Penelope threw her arm across Walt to prevent her from stepping onto the main street and colliding with a pair of boys chasing hoops. "Grace." After they and a cart of tanned hides had passed, she stepped into the lane. "Rose did not elope, and there was no captain."

"Then why'd you have me traipse up and down the county searching for good ole Franny?" Walt swiped an apple from a barrel in a passing cart. "Or dear brother John."

When the fruit was just inches from becoming her assistant's breakfast, Penelope snatched it, twirled around, and replaced it in the barrel. "Because I had to be certain."

Walt crossed her arms and muttered two or three rude words; however, as Penelope's brisk pace only widened the distance between them, she soon relented and jogged to catch her.

Once Walt was at her side once more, she continued. "From the beginning, there was more evidence in favour of a fake fiancé than any other theory." Penelope produced a satchel of candied nuts and dried fruits, which she handed to her assistant.

"How so?" Walt mumbled.

They paused where the forest lane met the high street to permit several carts to pass. Though the gentry were still abed or lounging in their drawing rooms, the working class were awake. It was a blur of browns and tans, "good morrows" and curses. As they stepped into the cobblestone square, Penelope asked, "Would you prefer I present it as a list or a paragraph?"

A man on horseback galloping in their direction recoiled from Walt's stare, that or the pistol she might have flashed. His horse missed them narrowly. "A list will suffice."

"Very well. No mention of a captain or a man in her diary. Unless, of course, you consider a yeti a man, which I do, especially after having met one."

Walt opened her mouth to ask a question but was overrun by Penelope's enthusiasm.

"No letters." She ticked off on her fingers. "No dirty novels."

Walt grabbed Penelope's elbow, bringing them to a halt. "None?"

Penelope shook her head, ignoring the shocked look on a passing lady's face as she covered her newborn babe's ears in horror.

"Not one." She continued, steering them towards the narrow alleys and road that led away from the public face of Alderwood, put on for visitors, to the heart of the town. "No suspicions by her mama."

Heading in her direction, Penelope spotted Harriet Greene, the physician's loose-lipped maid. As she was attired as herself and not as her alternative persona, Prudence Clearwater, the maid's eager eyes slid past her, focusing on a window displaying poke bonnets. Penelope reminded herself to visit the girl soon, both to hear gossip and to add to the girl's pocket money.

"No whispers among the staff," Penelope continued. "In all, no evidence that Rose Pilkington was involved in a tryst with anyone, let alone a captain."

"So then why pretend to elope?" They stood before an unmarked door. The odour of incense permeated the wood and wafted into the alleyway.

"To disappear." Penelope turned to Walt. "It is no coincidence that just weeks prior to her departure for London and days before a proposal from Mr Montagu, she would mysteriously vanish."

"Cold feet."

"Doubtful. Girls of Rose's standing do not forge nor abandon courtships without cause. A failed courtship would have wreaked havoc on her reputation, and though her father was wealthy and she might have recovered, it would have damaged her prospects for an advantageous match irrevocably." Penelope's eye lingered on the grimy door latch. She hesitated. Her assistant, aware of her hatred of dirt, pushed past her, turned the knob, and stepped inside.

"Yet another reason to steer clear of the marriage market," Walt whispered. A cavernous back-alley shop unfolded before them. As there were no windows, the fire on the hearth and a couple of lamps struggled to illuminate the space. The two women dodged bouquets of dried flowers and herbs hanging from the rafters.

Walt eyed her employer as though to ask, *What the blazes are we doin' here?*

A shrug would have to suffice, for it was the only reply Penelope gave. As no healer presented herself, they took seats at the table near the fireplace, but not before she swept the crumbs from her chair with her handkerchief.

The assistant leaned back, hands behind her head. "If she did not elope—"

"Since," Penelope interrupted in a hushed tone.

"*If!*" She pursed her lips in protest, yet lowered her volume. Who knew what lurked in the shadows of the room? "*If* she did not elope, then what happened? Kidnapped?"

"Kidnappers usually leave ransom notes, not misleading letters." Penelope studied the containment boxes placed about the room. What manner of talismans they held, she could only imagine. Ripping her gaze away from a blackened chest with a silver latch, she continued in a low tone, "That night, she discovered a secret that terrified her enough to pack her clothing in a rush."

"Come now, you cannot expect me to believe you could determine she had packed a bag in haste."

"Of course I can."

Walt crossed her arms. Challenge extended.

Penelope smirked. Challenge accepted. "Left her diary and a book under her bed, but packed her treasured novels and jewellery."

"How do you know she only packed the treasured ones?" Walt shot back.

"Because there were gaps on her shelf where novels had been removed." The sleuth gestured as though the shelves stood before her. "They were alphabetised, which indicates that she enjoys reading and that she selected specific novels. Finally . . ."

"There is more?" Walt tried not to grin and yet did. As a gambling woman, she appreciated a well-played hand.

"Finally, she packed an insufficient number of undergarments. A common mistake among those not used to packing their own clothing." She leaned back, victorious.

In unison, their heads turned to the archway leading to a second room. From the inky interior emerged a woman, a kindly matron who looked as though she had been baking scones. A warm smile revealed a mouth half-full of teeth. She wiped her hands on her flower-embroidered apron.

When the woman, no taller than a ten-year-old, leaned in, Penelope whispered a few words in her ear. A mischievous glint revealed that beneath the veil of baked goods and grey hair lay a woman who had a proclivity for the sinister.

She shuffled away and returned moments later with a vial and a sewing basket. After a quick exchange of coin and a farewell, the two women emerged into the alley once more.

Walt appraised her employer. "So, why'd Rose flee?"

"I presume it is linked to Grace's murder." Since Walt was along for the metaphorical ride, Penelope directed their steps towards the outskirts of Alderwood.

"Bumped her off, did she?"

"Doubtful, though possible." She hopped over a puddle, careful not to dirty her "town" boots or the hem of the muslin gown that hung straight as a column on her curveless frame. "No, I think she either found the body and guessed the murderer's identity . . ." She dodged a pile of horse droppings as they turned onto a country lane. ". . . or witnessed the murder itself."

A hedge of tall grass proved too tempting for Walt. Despite the impropriety, she plucked a yellow sheath, stuck it in her mouth, and chewed. "So, did Rose stage the tea?"

"Likely. And without the kitchen staff's help, I would presume." Penelope, much to her assistant's chagrin, ignored the provocation.

"Why, because of the missing sugar?"

"Precisely." Rows of black earth crowned with char-treuse buds radiated in every direction. The damp earth perfumed the air with a fragrance so pure it made Penelope heady. "A member of the staff could lay out a tray of tea things in his or her sleep; a spoilt girl could not."

Walt did not restrain a wry grin. "Calling the kettle black, aren't you, Miss Pot."

Penelope kept her eyes locked on the parsonage in the distance, refusing to acknowledge Walt's comment, which, if truth were told, hit a tad close to home. "If Rose did witness Grace's murder or discover the body, then that would suggest she is familiar with and intimately connected to the murderer."

Her companion nodded. As they passed a knot of ladies, each with a sewing basket or bag tucked under their arm, Walt's cheeks blanched with dread. She sighed. "Which narrows it down to a half a dozen suspects at most."

"Yes, most of whom will be at the ball tonight."

"What of the rest of the suspects?" Their pace slowed as they approached the dry stone wall encircling the parsonage, a proper English cottage with a neat garden and a white arch to welcome visitors. "Want me to interrogate them?"

"Not necessary." With care, Penelope adjusted her bonnet trimmed with tasteful lace and silk dahlias.

"Why not?"

"Well, because one is . . ." A pair of ladies approached. Penelope nodded a greeting. ". . . dead, and another, Mrs Bates, the Pilkingtons' housekeeper, just so happens to be a creature of habit."

"She's inside the parsonage, in't she?" To describe Walt's expression as annoyed would be an understatement. It appeared she had been unknowingly roped into attending a gathering of ladies. Ugh! It was a wonder she did not flee into the fields.

"Yes." Our sadistic heroine beamed. "On Mondays, Mrs Bates sees to purchases in town and attends this sewing circle." With that, she held open the gate, gesturing for Walt to enter.

As she passed, Walt flashed a gesture of her own.

# CHAPTER 23
## The Chapter with Too Much Truth Telling

"Lord Proby rose for the purpose of introducing
into the Bill a clause for preventing the prosecution
of military officers and members of the judiciary
for the use of truth tinctures without express
permission. As per the Law Governing Magic and
Magickind of 1798, all other applications shall be
forbidden."

*Magic Act of 1812*

{Narrator's Note: The events of the sewing
circle on the eighth of April 1811 went down in
infamy. Though no formal inquiries were made
into the matter, as all present denied that anything
untoward had occurred, the aftermath of that day
reverberated throughout the kingdom and led to
the almost unanimous passage of the Magic Act of
1812.

Rumour has it that it all went awry when the tea
was served.}

By a hurried set of whispered directives, Penelope instructed Walt to slip a couple of drops of truth tincture into Mrs Bates's tea. Having secured the seat nearest the housekeeper, our sleuth withdrew a needlepoint from the basket she had borrowed from the herbalist and began to sew.

Conversations around the circle were commonplace enough—marriages, engagements, and children. How dull. Focused as she was both on not stabbing herself and on gleaning useful information, Penelope had not noticed that Walt had served the tea. As she was unknown, no one baulked at the offer. If the ladies even noticed her as she noiselessly moved about the room, they likely assumed she was someone else's cousin.

First, Mrs Bates was served, then Penelope. An almost imperceptible shake of her head and a knowing glance from Walt indicated to her that she ought not to drink the tea. Instead, she rested it on the table beside her, but not before pouring half of its contents into an obliging houseplant.

"Miss Sedgewick, how lovely it is for you to join us today. It has been three weeks at least." Mrs Bates was the picture of an English housekeeper—hair swept into a tidy bun with wisps of grey at the temples, a silver pocket watch clipped to her apron, and a steely gaze that kept a household of staff in line. In other words, she was worth her weight in gold.

Eager not to betray herself or her assistant, Penelope kept her eyes trained on her sewing pattern. "Four, in fact." *Or five, maybe even six.* "I have longed to rejoin the circle. I find the conversation diverting and the company . . ." *informative* ". . . delightful."

Mrs Bates lifted her cup and saucer and raised it to chest height. Penelope watched as she . . . lowered the cup and saucer to her lap to chat with her dear friend and hostess, the parson's wife. Drat!

Around the circle, half a dozen ladies chit-chatted, sipped their tea and even made time to sew; after all, it is universally known that clubs and societies exist for the sake of gossip, not for sewing cushions. The room, while respectable and tidy, was not spacious. The circle accommodated the dozen attendees by bringing in a few chairs from the dining room.

A lady seated across from Penelope sipped her tea while smiling at her friend, a baroness, who wore a shocking shade of mauve and bright rouge on her cheeks. To her left, a pair of middle-aged twin old maids dressed in matching canary yellow exchanged knowing glances. Nearly everyone had drunk from their cups.

Penelope began to fidget. The look of glee radiating from Walt's face unsettled her. If Mrs Bates did not drink her tea, and soon, the opportunity to question her about the basket might pass, for the housekeeper was shrewd and would guess the cause of an outbreak of unwarranted mass honesty.

Thankfully, Fate must have been as invested in the solving of Grace's murder as you and I, for at that moment, Mrs Bates made the mistake of biting into one of the parson's wife's scones, which were known to be as dry as a mouthful of cinnamon. Though she grinned as she chewed the moisture-wicking monstrosity, she raised her cup and downed half of its contents. Penelope breathed a sigh of relief.

"Mrs Bates," she began, leaning in to ensure she was heard. "I heard about the unfortunate death of the maid. I trust that the household is weathering it well."

"Oh yes." She mirrored Penelope and drew closer to her. "A few of the silly chits thought her ghost was wandering the halls, but I soon squashed that nonsense."

Though tempted, Penelope did not grin, nor did she stand on the couch and dance with delight. The healer was worth every penny. Her elegant concoction of truth tincture and a relaxant blended with a few drops of focus fog was superbly done. Not only would Mrs Bates willingly answer her questions without her usual guardedness, but she would forget she ever had or, at least, not remember whether or not she had. Splendid!

"Well done." She noted that the pitch of the conversation had risen an octave. Penelope raised her teacup to toast the housekeeper. "Have there been any inquiries into her death?"

"No, not one." The effects of the tincture were evident. Mrs Bates, usually skilled at needlepoint, had begun to stab at it haphazardly. "I believe the girl might have been foxed." She tapped the side of her nose and winked. "Who trips over a rug unless they are top-heavy? Hmm?"

"Who indeed?"

The potency of the tincture was evident in the lack of focus of the housekeeper's eyes and the slur of her words. The twins and the baroness wore faces that mirrored Mrs Bates, as did every other lady around the room. With the exception of Walt, who stood in the corner near hysterics.

As whatever happened next would only be remembered as a muddied daydream, Penelope cut to the chase. "Who requested tea to be served to the parlour that evening?"

"No one, at least not to the best of my knowledge." Mrs Bates pricked her finger and swore. "The butler, the steward, and I could not determine who had requested it, though it could have been Miss Pilkington. She disappeared that evening."

"You told me you thought we looked lovely in yellow," one of the twins grumbled through gritted teeth to the lady beside her.

"I lied." She crossed her arms. "You look like a pair of ducklings."

Sensing that the situation might devolve into a brawl, Penelope turned her attention to Mrs Bates once more. "I thought she went to visit a cousin. Did she not?"

"Bah!" The housekeeper sloshed her cup, spilling a few droplets on her skirt; she paid them no mind. "There is not a thing in that house that I do not know of. In fact . . ." She signalled for Penelope to lean in, which she did. ". . . when her parents were away, she often sneaked off into the woods unaccompanied."

Penelope, in mock horror, placed her hand on her chest. "No! How extraordinary."

"Yes! And that evening, I saw her slip into the forest myself. Alone. Carrying her own bags."

"No!" She held her cup to her lips and, careful not to allow the liquid to touch her mouth, pretended to sip. "Whatever business could a young lady have in the forest at night?"

"Spill the tea, you say? Darling, I am the tea." the baroness in mauve boasted. All eyes turned in her direction.

"I can't help it if her son prefers the arms of an experienced woman to all of the dim-witted girls she parades past him!" She rose, triumphant, glaring at the poor mama. "Yes! It all started as a brush last year, yet since he is—"

"Skilled at the feather-bed jig!" added one of the twins with a knowing look in her eye.

"And more!" The baroness collected her basket. "I intend to continue our affair and may even marry him." With that, she stormed from the room, leaving her lover's mama in need of smelling salts.

Mrs Bates clutched her side, giggling like a schoolgirl. "This is the best sewing circle I have attended in a decade." She drained the rest of her cup.

"Not sure why most of you are thunderstruck." The second twin lifted her chin. "Half of the firstborn among you were 'premature'." She giggled.

A cursory glance around the room informed Penelope that the twin had struck a chord. Several of the ladies had either shaded the colour of a ripe tomato or appeared as though they were having a fit.

"And," the lady continued. "One of your children . . ." Her chin angled towards a lady near the window who was known for penning pamphlets on the dangers of drink. ". . . bears a striking resemblance to her husband's dearest friend, a prominent member of His Majesty's Privy Counsel."

Penelope, fearing their time would be cut short by a riot, pressed on. "Miss Pilkington stole into the forest, you say? Do you think she had a beau?"

"Could have, but doubtful. Of late, her eye lingered on Frank—"

"The footman?"

The corner of Mrs Bates's mouth tugged upward. Apparently, even middle-aged women found Frank irresistible. "Yes, Frank the footman. Caused the mistress a great deal of discomfort. Had Frank not had enough sense to ignore her glances and giggles, it would have cost him his job."

Penelope felt the temperature of the room change as several ladies crimsoned, either in anger or in shame, as increasingly salacious secrets were spilt. Walt, still hiding in the corner, was beside herself.

The time had come to be blunt. "Who told you to send the basket to Grace's brother?"

"I found a note the next morning instructing me to have one delivered anonymously." Mrs Bates's eyes darted between the twins, who looked near to blows. "It was written in the mistress's hand."

Penelope could have done a cartwheel. And would have, had not a resounding *SMACK!* drawn the eye of the sewing circle. A knight's wife clutched her cheek while the parson's wife, face flushed, hair dishevelled, hand raised, bellowed, "My scones are NOT dry, you . . . {This word has been removed by the editors; however, the reader may insert whatever curse they see fit}."

Sensing that a brawl was about to erupt, Penelope ushered the ladies homewards, hoping the walk would provide sufficient time for the effects of the tincture to dissipate. After having parted from Mrs Bates at the gate, she wandered towards her own home. Her eyes roved the path and fields for Walt. She discovered her leaning against a signpost near a fork in the road, arms crossed, glowing with mischief.

"Best—Sewing—Circle—Ever." She fell into step beside her employer. "If they were all like that, I would become a regular member."

Unsure whether she ought to congratulate Walt on her skilled mischief-making or censure her for the chaos that ensued, Penelope chose to do neither, allowing a tut and pursed lips to serve as her response before turning her feet homewards.

# CHAPTER 24

## The Chapter with Too Much Dancing

*"That exercise is as essential to the preservation
of health as pure air or wholesome food, is a fact
so generally known and admitted that it needs no
comment whatever."*

*An Analysis of Country Dancing, 1808*

Balls were the epitome of polite society in 1811—the dancing, the music, the dresses—or so the novels would have us believe. In reality, they were often exhaustingly sweaty affairs that culminated in dashed hopes and injured toes. Penelope would have avoided them entirely had they not been such furtive soil for gossip.

At nine, they arrived, Penelope on her uncle's arm. He would wander to one of the rooms set aside for the gentlemen. Among the throng were a few acquaintances eager to discuss science or history with the aid of his valet, who occasionally interpreted for him when quill and paper were too inconvenient a medium for discourse.

He patted her hand before he released it. "Try to enjoy yourself, my dear."

"I shall try." She kissed him on the cheek before being swept into the ballroom.

A throng of butterflies swirling in the wind under a sea of starlight: that was the impression the ballroom made on Penelope that evening. The white columns reminded her of birches, holding the ceiling aloft. Rather than branches weighed down by leaves, curtains swayed in the breeze let in at the windows.

Before she leapt into the intrigue, she stood for a moment, her sprite-like frame elongated by her white chiffon gown with golden embroidery at the neck, hem, and sleeves. With her sable hair woven intricately into a knot and her mother's pearls adorning her neck, she drew the eye of more than a few passing gentlemen, and not for the size of her inheritance or her name alone.

Her hazel eyes shone like amber under the light of the chandeliers. She had but one aim: to dance with Sir Lawrence Pilkington.

With care, she avoided the smiles of half a dozen gentlemen. A blank dance card suited her better than a full one, and even at twenty-seven, nearly an old maid in most men's books, she found that her wealth attracted more attention than she wished.

Unfortunately, the curled, auburn hair of Sir Lawrence was absent from the dance floor. Nor was he near the punch table. And, to her dismay, he was not at the door, greeting his guests. She even nipped into the hallway near the card room, hoping to spot him there. Nothing. Not a hint of the knight.

Perturbed, she swept into the ballroom once more, determined. She would dance with Sir Lawrence. How else could she entrap the man for twenty minutes?

Politeness would press him into conversation while propriety would prevent him from escaping.

As Penelope stood on her tiptoes, her eyes roving the room, Mrs Stevenson approached with a general on her arm. Her golden gown draped across her curves in a manner that would have sent an artist's heart aflutter. Then again, the depth to which her neckline plunged—dancing the line between improper and scandalous—would have caused cardiac irregularities in most men.

The flash of an uncharacteristically toothy smile brought Mrs Stevenson to a halt opposite Penelope. The adroit general greeted a friend, leaving the ladies to converse. Given his years of experience fighting battles, he probably sensed that such a smile was tantamount to a dragon baring its teeth.

She curtseyed. "Good evening, Mrs Stevenson. It is lovely to see you."

"And you as well." Mrs Stevenson eyed her, puzzled. That is, until she caught sight of Penelope's necklace. A gentleness curbed the voluptuousness of her features. "Are those your mother's pearls?"

"They are." Penelope's fingers danced across them.

"They suit." Her mouth curled into a grin. "You remind me of her. Your aunt and I discuss it often."

Not willing to be capsized by anything as silly as sentimentality, Penelope shoved the rising tightness in her throat aside, stomped on it, and scheduled a time to revisit it next year (or the year after). Composed once more, she asked, "Have you seen . . ."

Across the ballroom strode Sir Lawrence, not with his wife, nor with a viscountess, but with Walt. With a spring in his step and his head held high enough to scrape the ceiling, he led her to the dance floor. Blast!

Turning once more to Mrs Stevenson, she grabbed her hand. "Imusthaveapartnerforthefirstdance."

Mrs Stevenson fluttered her lashes in an attempt to comprehend. "Come again."

Penelope, determined to behave like a rational being, steadied herself. "Would you be so kind as to help me procure a partner for the first dance?"

"Of course." Her gaze lingered for a moment, communicating, *I expect an explanation.* As providence would have it, the curate, a young man with pleasing manners and little sense, passed near. "Mr——"

{Reader, as Penelope was distracted by the musicians taking their seats, she missed the gentleman's name. He shall, therefore, be referred to as Mr U for unknown. Carry on.}

"My dear friend, Miss Sedgewick has informed me that you two are not yet acquainted."

The pitiable curate was stunned—stunned speechless, if we are being precise. After all, it was not every day that a woman of Mrs Stevenson's calibre addressed a country curate to introduce him to the wealthiest eligible lady in the county. He sputtered a string of words resembling, "A pleasure to make your acquaintance."

A curtsey and a bow were exchanged. Through a series of expert manoeuvres and a bit of coaxing, the bewildered Mr U led our heroine to the dance floor under the gobsmacked gazes of half the room.

Intent on standing beside Walt, Penelope tugged the sod onward. Sir Lawrence stood near the head of the line, opposite his partner, salivating. Walt, who was intentionally ignoring the line of dribble on his chin, resembled a field of daisies in her white organza gown with pearls pinned in her spiral locks.

Pair after pair stepped forward to dance, eager to claim the places near the front of the line. Penelope steered her partner past three couples too befuddled by love or lust to pay them any mind. Whether she intentionally stepped on a lady's hem to gain ground is uncertain, though likely, considering the pleased expression on her face. The final couple was overtaken when the gentleman unexpectedly stumbled (or tripped on her slipper). Pity.

Winded, the hapless curate assumed his position opposite her in the line while she pasted a pleasant expression on her face. Sir Lawrence acknowledged her with a nod. The curate, still thunderstruck, stared at her. And Walt feigned as though she did not exist.

Unable to question Walt, she surveyed the room. One couple after another took their place in the line until it stretched to the far end of the room. It reminded her of a garden. The ladies' dresses, gleaming like iridescent petals, swayed to the melody of conversation. Gentlemen filled the role of bees, buzzing expectantly in dark coats. Even those who did not dance bowed and curtseyed like tulips bouncing on a breeze. A picturesque scene, or so it would be if she knew what the blazes Walt intended.

"Lady Pilkington—" Blazes! The curate. Penelope turned to him. Appearances must be preserved, after all. "—has invited the ideal number of guests, has she not?"

"Indeed, she has." She adjusted the strand of pearls at her neck. After she had spent half of her first Season sneezing, she had paid dearly to have them imbued with a dampening charm. While it robbed her of the ability to sense the presence of magic, it was a calculated risk she willingly took. Besides, drakes and unicorns rarely wandered into ballrooms.

When the first chords were played, a ripple of expectation pulsed down the line. Men preened. Ladies glowed. Penelope scoffed. Dancing, in her opinion, ought to be reserved for lovers, not indifferent acquaintances. Ugh! She loathed chitchat as much as disorganization and blisters.

Curtsies and bows were exchanged. The gentlemen began the dance by crossing towards their partners. When Sir Lawrence and Mr U circled them to return to their positions, she muttered through clenched teeth, "What the blazes are you doing here?"

"Helping." Walt lifted her chin towards the ceiling before continuing in an accent that would have fooled even a duchess. "Or do you not wish me to discover whether Sir Lawrence's travels correspond with the dates in Grace's journal?"

As it was their turn to cross together and circle their partners, Penelope was forced to mask her shame by screwing her heart-shaped mouth into a semblance of a smile, yet not too eager a one, lest she mislead the pitiable Mr U.

Once they had swept past their partners, she whispered, "I misjudged you. I apologize."

Walt would doubtlessly lord her confession over her at a later time. Until then, she floated towards her partner like the pappus of a dandelion carried on the wind. Her buttery voice began, "My aunt and I attended the ball last September. Had you been in attendance—"

"Books," interjected Mr U. "Which do you prefer?"

Crap! Him. Again. His inopportune attentions had distracted her. Her conscience wagged its proverbial finger. *Be polite.* "Oh, there are so many." *Do not rattle on about science.* "I could never decide. What are your preferences?"

The pair parted after they had woven a crisscrossed path with Sir Lawrence and Walt. Careful not to race, Penelope peeled away to join hands with her friend and another lady. Under her breath, she pressed, "What did he reply?"

"Thus far, I have discovered that he was away frequently during September and October, which would have aligned with . . ." The choreography carried Walt away to her partner and his fawning once more. Penelope, though, put two and two together. Sir Lawrence had been absent often last autumn, which coincided with the dates in Grace's journal. If Walt could—

"Fordyce!" The curate spoke with a tad too much enthusiasm. He shaded the colour of a strawberry. "Fordyce's Sermons," he restated sheepishly as he took her hand. "Have you read them?"

Penelope's lips began to curl of their own volition. Of course she had read them—to eviscerate them, naturally. A series of sweeps and flutters led her away from Mr U, providing a welcome opportunity for her to compose herself. That is, until she discerned the sound of Sir Lawrence's voice. "No, I was away in . . ."

"Lovely!" A matron who stood near squawked. "Most handsome gi—" The stare Penelope levelled in her direction silenced the interrupter (as well as half of the room), and though she could hear the cadence of the knight's voice, his words were swallowed by the crescendo of the strings.

Her partner drew near, forcing her to reply, "Yes, I have indeed read them. They were. . ." *a pitiful example of poorly reasoned arguments weaponized to coerce young women into "proper" behaviour* ". . . enlightening."

"And in November . . ." Penelope strained her ear to overhear Walt as she passed, but, as fortune was decidedly set against her that day, a gentleman resembling a barrel coughed, drowning out her voice.

The rest of the dance proceeded in a similar fashion— the curate introducing a topic, Penelope resisting the urge to scoff, Walt posing a question, and Sir Lawrence muttering a reply. Torturous.

When the final chords rang across the room and the gentlemen had been dismissed to fetch their partners a glass of punch, Walt drew her into an embrace and whispered, "His journeys coincide with the entries in Grace's journal, save for the one in January. I was unable to question him on those dates without arousing his suspicions."

"Thank you." Penelope pressed her hand as she stepped away. As Walt's attentions were claimed by a gaggle of hopefuls, she permitted herself to be swept into the stream of ladies circulating the room in search of Sir Lawrence.

Penelope had every intention of securing a dance with him—that is, until the characteristic sound of her uncle's voice rising over the din drew her eye across the dance floor. There, in the doorway opposite, she spotted him being escorted towards the main entrance by a constable.

Throwing decorum to the wind, Penelope broke into a run. She shoved through the dancers, weaving frantically towards the hall. When she burst into it, a crowd had gathered, every head turned towards the entrance. Blind to the gasps and stares of others, she pressed through the throng until she reached the front door.

On the steps outside stood Uncle Archie. Though his face was flat, the concern reflected in his eyes mirrored hers. Beside him stood his valet.

As she crossed the last few yards between them, she signed, "What is happening?"

Uncle Archie tugged a mask of calm over his features. "A simple misunderstanding, that is all. I shall sort it out."

She looked to his valet, who was dressed impeccably. Ever the faithful servant, he kept his hands clasped behind his back and his lips firmly pressed into a line.

Desperate, she turned to the magistrate, who had only just arrived in his carriage. He alighted, not dressed for a ball but in a black coat for travel. Its dark colours highlighted the contours of his carved face.

"Sir." She curtseyed, willing her hands not to shake. "What is the meaning of this?"

He did not answer. Rather, his coal-pit eyes shot past her. A moment later, her aunt was at her side, weaving a hand through the crook of her arm. They waited, a sense of foreboding pressing against their chests.

The magistrate bowed, then signalled for the men to load her uncle into his carriage. "Your uncle has been named as a suspect by the inquest investigating the death of Mr Montagu."

# CHAPTER 25

## The Chapter with Hope

"True hope is swift, and flies with swallow's wings.
Kings it makes gods, and meaner creatures kings."

*Shakespeare, Richard III*

For the second day in a row, Penelope rose before the sunrise. On this occasion, however, no toothy grin greeted her. Instead, a familiar buttermilk canopy framed her room. Opposite her, the dwindling embers of last night's fire flickered in the fireplace. A chill hung in the air.

She crossed to the windows and flung open the curtains. A light brighter than a million candles blazed on the horizon. Her eye traced the familiar landscape—the wild forest and the tidy garden—avoiding the paths where she and Uncle Archie would wander.

It was there he had taught her to use a skipping rope as a girl. Under the arches of ivy, he had held her when they had learnt of her parents' deaths. His coat had smelt of cinnamon. She had buried her face in the rough fabric, willing them alive, yet knowing it could not be.

186

Her throat constricted. A torrent of heat crashed through her body. She craved to move, yet she could not; to flee, yet her body was paralyzed. A wild, guttural sob burst from her before she clapped her hand over her mouth, stifling it.

She would not give way.

She could not.

She must save him.

So she dressed, pretending her hands did not tremble, and left her room.

When she opened the library door, she half expected it to reveal her uncle in his usual seat with Cerberus beside him and his plate teetering on a pile of journals. The sight of his vacant chair threatened to drag forth a sob once more.

Her aunt occupied her usual seat, wearing black, as always. An additional chair had been added for Mrs Stevenson. The ladies greeted her with kind smiles, their faces each bearing signs of their own private grief.

Ambrose's chair sat vacant. She spied his sandy scales curled protectively around Cerberus's brilliant coral tones. Neither lifted their head when she entered.

The thought of eating made her stomach churn, but for the sake of her uncle, she could not afford to go hungry. She served herself a lone piece of honey bread and buttered it before drizzling honey in a zig-zag pattern across the top—just as her uncle would.

The clink of the cutlery against their plates grated on Penelope as she poured herself a cup of tea. It would have been polite for her to refill the other cups. Yet she could not; the tremor had returned when she spotted her uncle's scrawl in the margin of a newspaper.

"So," her aunt began. She patted her lips with her napkin, not the edge of the tablecloth as was preferred in some households. "Seated at this table are two of the most brilliant minds in the whole of England, as well as one superior to the average." Aunt Josephine reached across the table to squeeze her friend's hand. "No offence, my dear. Your other qualities more than compensate."

Mrs Stevenson, her milky skin paler than usual, merely shrugged and continued to butter her toast.

Penelope bit into her bread, washing it down with a sip of tea. The tangy flavour on her tongue, cut by the smoky sweetness of the honey, reassured her. "Yesterday . . ." Her voice cracked. She drained her cup, leaving only the fannings swirling in the bottom. "Yesterday, I discovered the body of Mr Montagu just after sunrise."

Her aunt paused, her hands suspended, hovering over the handle of the teapot she had reached for. "And why—"

"Why did I not mention this last night?"

Behind her aunt's crystal eyes swirled a million questions.

Mrs Stevenson brushed her friend's hands aside and reached for the pot to fill each cup with care. "Is it not obvious, Jo? Had she come forward, it would have incriminated Archibald rather than exonerated him."

A dip of the chin was Aunt Josephine's sole reply. Like Penelope, her aunt was weaving this information into her web of theories.

Penelope, with the level of precision expected by her aunt, described the scene and the state of the body, omitting (obviously) the bit about listening to the pistol. After all, she could not disclose Mr Montagu's duel with the farmer—who, according to the intelligence provided by the physician's maid, Harriet, had survived his injuries—without disclosing that she possessed a gift.

"So, the body had been moved?" Mrs Stevenson asked.

Aunt Josephine nodded. "And the murder took place indoors?"

"Yes, and . . ."

Cerberus lifted her head. An alertness unheard of for the hour roused her. Her frill stood on end. A nudge of her wing stirred Ambrose as well. He nodded his head before they bounded from the chair to the door.

Before the humans could render aid, the faedragon, no larger than a bunny, fluttered her wings and turned the knob. The pair raced into the hall in the direction of the front entrance.

Aunt Josephine began to rise, her hands pressed into the table. She looked to her friend for support. Half hope, half dread swirled in Penelope, anchoring to her chair.

The tip, tap of a dragon's nails on the hardwood announced their return. Moments later, the door swung open to reveal Uncle Archie, rumpled, as usual, and unharmed. "What did I—"

The remainder of his question was knocked out of him when his niece, followed by his sister, launched themselves into his arms. Penelope buried her face in his coat, drinking in the lingering odours of chalk dust and cinnamon. With one hand, he pulled her close as though afraid to let her go.

When she released him and stepped back, no tears lingered on her lashes, not even one. She held his gaze, cherishing the deep lines that radiated from his smile like rays of sunlight. Tears spilt down his rough cheek. Penelope brushed one away with her thumb before leading him to his chair.

A plate piled high with his favourite treats was laid before him, courtesy of Mrs Stevenson. Once he was seated, Cerberus hopped into his lap. He burst into laughter when she peppered his face with kisses before fluttering to her own chair, where Ambrose awaited her.

A sip of tea and a bite of cake later, and he set aside his fork. His brow sank into a deep furrow. He signed, "They have not dropped the allegations against me."

Of course they had not. His niece and friend, though downcast, were not surprised. It was his sister, strangling the tablecloth in her fists, who lowered her head, a pained look of defeat clouding her face.

Faithful Mrs Stevenson asked the question her friend could not. "Why do they believe you shot him? What evidence could they have against you?"

"It is circumstantial at best. Yesterday morning, I was out walking." Uncle Archie paused to take up his cup. His weathered hands cradled it. He rocked it gently, watching as the umber liquid broke like waves on the sides before he returned it to its saucer. "Supposedly, a farmer spotted me cutting through the field near where his body was discovered."

Penelope's heart crumpled under the weight of the revelation; had she not been eager to flee the scene and had she delivered the letter herself, he would not have ventured out that morning.

"But it is your own field!" her aunt burst out. "Has not a man the right to walk his own grounds?" Her face had drained of colour, a stark contrast to her black gown. This

190

was not the hellbent fury she exercised against the cruel or the selfish; this was a desperation Penelope had never witnessed. It unnerved her more than anything else had, for if her aunt, with all of her strength and cunning, had lost faith, what hope remained?

Uncle Archie took her hand, as did her friend.

"There is more. Last week, at Viscount Montagu's estate, I joined Lord Alderwood and a few others in a game of cards."

"You play cards?" and "You were in the same room as Lord Alderwood?" were signed simultaneously by Mrs Stevenson and Penelope.

"Yes." A nervous grin quivered on his lips. Even though he had been accused of murder, he, like most men, likely preferred that his uptight older sister not discover that he occasionally bet on cards. "During the game, I realised that young Mr Montagu was cheating. I alerted Lord Alderwood, who had lost a great sum to the pup."

"That alone is not cause to suspect you of murder," asserted Aunt Josephine, more sure, less discouraged than before.

"It does if he shoved me then spat in my face, as well as insulting me, calling me addled."

Any sympathy Penelope had had for Mr Montagu vanished. Had she known he had called her uncle such hateful words, she would have dispatched him herself when they had met in the field not two days prior. They would have been spared the heartache, and the field dragons would have enjoyed a snack.

Uncle Archie stroked Cerberus's head. "When his parents learnt of his death, they travelled by dragon to his

191

brother's estate. Lord Alderwood informed me by letter that one or two of the party that evening were questioned. Given the Montagus' position and the pressure exerted by his parents, the constable felt forced into making an arrest. As it is nearly Easter, if the grand jury finds the case compelling tomorrow, it will be set to be tried by the Court of Assizes on Friday."

"Friday?" Her aunt extracted a blank piece of foolscap from the mound of sketches. The straightness of her shoulders told Penelope that she had regained her composure. "Well, then, where do we begin?

Penelope did not attend as the facts were outlined; she could not. A match had been struck in the corner of her mind. She closed off her senses, retreating from the light filtering through the window, the lilt of voices, the sensation of the tepid tea swirling over her tongue.

A spiderweb of facts formed in her mind. As it did, she found the final piece of the missing puzzle. As it slipped snugly into its spot, the picture became complete, or nearly so.

While her aunt, uncle, and friend continued to talk, comparing theories and discussing strategies, a resolve solidified within Penelope; she knew what must be done to save her uncle. Afraid to give false hope, she listened patiently, waiting for the party to break up.

When it did, she yanked her uncle into a hug and, because she knew he would not hear her, whispered, "I shall set this to right, I swear." With that, she turned and practically raced down the front steps.

# CHAPTER 26

## The Chapter with the Torn Pages

"The peerage system is headed by the dukes,
followed by marquesses, earls, viscounts, and
barons. The final rung is occupied by baronets and
knights, who are honoured with the distinction
of being hereditary and honorary knights,
respectively."

*The Peerage System: A Commentary, page 34*

Walt had only shot at nine people in her lifetime, and all
of them were men. However, on the ninth of April, she
considered adding a woman to the list and making it an
even ten.

> {Narrator's Note: To be clear, Walt had never
> murdered anyone (probably). She had merely
> maimed a couple of men.}

Despite the ghastly hour (seven thirty), Penelope
flung the door to her office open with such force that
two picture frames came clattering to the ground.
Without a "Hello" or a "Pardon" or even an "Oi!" she

charged to the bookshelf and began running her fingers across the bindings, muttering to herself. Her hand paused occasionally to straighten a stray tome to align with the others.

When Walt emerged, her hair resembled a starling's nest after a windstorm. Her hand was tucked into the pocket of her bottle-green banyan, a loose robe generally reserved for men. Whether the pocket concealed a weapon is of no import, for it was the scowl on her face that could have killed. "Whatcha doin' 'ere ye ninny'ead?"

"Until you address me in intelligible English, I shall presume that you have wished me a good morning." Penelope did not turn, which was just as well, considering the string of unladylike gestures Walt brandished in her direction. "Have you seen Grace's journal?"

Met with silence, she turned to observe Walt stuffing her hands into her pockets hastily.

Without a word, her assistant disappeared into the bedroom and emerged with the fabric volume in question. She unceremoniously let it fall to the desktop, toppling a candlestick, before flopping into her chair.

Without commenting on her posture, Penelope hurried to the desk.

Whether it was the pinched look on her employer's face, the fact that she ignored the fallen candlestick, or the way she nearly tore the pages from the binding as she flipped through them, Walt opened a single eye to appraise her. "Are you alright, miss?"

"Of course," she answered in a clipped tone. "Fine. I am fine."

Walt rose and meandered over to the desk to stand opposite her. "You sure about that?"

"Why would I not be?" She slammed one page against another, tearing the corner.

Her assistant shrugged before stepping behind the shade to dress for the day. "No reason."

"Just because I may have solved Grace's murder." Another page slapping against the next echoed

"And discovered the identity of her lover." *SLAP!* "And may be the cause of my uncle's predicament."

Walt poked her head out from behind the shade. "What predicament?"

*SLAP!* "Oh, did I not mention it?" *SLAP!* "He is to be tried for the murder of Mr Montagu. Unless, of course, I can prove my theories correct, which is trying, given the state of our justice system and the fact that I, as a woman, am viewed not as an equal but as an appendage." *SLAP! SLAP! SLAP!* A page ripped from the binding. She cast it aside.

With her dress half-buttoned, Walt emerged. She wandered over to the desk, stood opposite her friend, and placed her hand on the open diary.

When Penelope looked up, she was not met with judgment—no, her friend's eyes conveyed a solidarity that nearly broke her.

"Sorry, miss. I know he is like a father to you."

"Better than." Penelope's throat cinched as she blinked away the wetness that threatened to tumble down her cheeks. "Walt, what if I cannot—"

"You will."

"But—"

"No buts."

They stood there, silent—the tidal wave of her fear shrinking under her friend's unyielding faith. Neither moved.

After some time, Penelope returned to flipping through the pages. "If only I could find—" Her hand hovered above a rose petal that Grace had hidden there. Two nights prior, in James's lodgings, she had listened to the note tucked into the journal. It had revealed nothing, but this . . . this could confirm the identity of the maid's lover, which, with any luck, could help Penelope solve two mysteries.

"What's a rose petal have to do with your uncle?" Though Walt's tone suggested a genuine curiosity, there again was that quizzical look as though Penelope were a puzzle she had not yet solved to her satisfaction.

Our heroine could have lied. She probably ought to have. It would have been the wiser course. After all, magic was all fine and well, but much like that vulgar new dance known as the waltz, or the education of women, it was best left to those who must earn their bread, certainly not ladies or heiresses. Not to mention that a quarter of the population despised the Folk and longed to rid the country of them.

However, whether it was desperation or common sense, as they are often one and the same, Penelope blurted, "I'm a sniffer and a listener."

Walt retrieved her jaw from the floor before she lowered herself into her chair. Methodically, she packed and lit her pipe. Penelope waited. The flavour of the smoke swirling in her mouth proved restorative.

"I never would've believed it. You . . ." She looked at her friend. ". . . used a contraction."

Penelope sputtered. "*That* is what you find astounding?"

"'Course. I figured you were a sniffer long ago. It's all that nose-crinkling you do. And though it's news that you're also a listener, I wouldn't call it shocking." She kicked her legs over the arm of her chair. "So, if you listening to that petal might save your uncle, have at it."

Her gaze flashed from the object in her hand to Walt and back again. The fragile, pale petal hummed, beckoning her.

No sooner had her eyes slid closed did the vision of Grace laughing spring to life. Against the landscape of white, her ginger hair shone like the sunset. Snowflakes clung to her hair and shoulders, shimmering like crystals. And, there, opposite her, stood her lover.

Penelope yanked herself from the vision, half-hysterical laughter bursting from her. She covered her mouth. "Walt, I was right."

"'Course you were." She returned to the bedroom to finish her toilette. "So, where are we off to this fine morning?"

"We?" Penelope dashed into the bedroom and yanked the drawer to the cabinet open with such vigour that two of the perfume bottles teetered and fell on their sides. She quickly righted them, careful to align them in neat rows once more before she pulled a sensible pale-blue dress from the drawer.

Walt stepped from behind the shade, her figure adding elegance to what otherwise would have been an unremarkable muslin gown. "Yes, *we*. You don't honestly believe I'd let you face this alone, do you?"

Our heroine paused midstride. A look passed between the ladies, communicating what they already knew: they were not employer and employee; they were friends. And not everyday friends, but the sort you would ride to the gates of hell with while cackling in delight.

She did not suppress the grin she felt, not even a little. How could she? As she stepped behind the curtain, she drew a steadying breath. "To the physician's home."

"What has he to do with Mr Montagu's murder?"

"Little, but . . ." Penelope crossed the room to retrieve the charm she sported when posing as Prudence Clearwater. ". . . his maid loves fine clothes and is easily bribed."

Walt shrugged. "Who isn't nowadays?"

# CHAPTER 26 1/2

## The Half Chapter

{Narrator's Note: As the last chapter was bordering on becoming a tad too long, the author has decided to experiment with half chapters. Please accept this note as both an epigraph and an apology for her unorthodox choice.}

Miss Harriet Greene, a loquacious young maid and purveyor of overheard conversations, answered the mint-green door leading to the physician's lodgings when she heard a knock at eight that morning. As she had expected it to be the delivery boy from the herbalist's shop and not two women, she scowled at Walt.

Upon spotting Prudence Clearwater, her entire demeanour underwent an alteration. To encounter a ready source of income twice in a week was a treat she had not anticipated.

Before stepping outside, she glanced skyward. Though it was overcast, a deluge did not appear to be an imminent threat to her coiffure. She slipped outside, closing the door gently behind her. "Morning, miss." She curtseyed. "How can I be of service today?"

Penelope pursed her lips, reminding herself that she was a secretary, not an heiress hellbent on clearing her uncle's name. "I had wondered if I might impose upon you." She fiddled with the fabric button on the sleeve of her spencer. "When we spoke last, you mentioned a duel. Do you recall?"

The shimmer of a half-crown reflected in Harriet's eyes as she imagined the silk stockings her information could buy. She leaned a shoulder against the white doorframe and crossed her arms. "Yes. I remember."

Rather than firing questions, Penelope tiptoed into the topic. "Did you happen to learn the name of the farmer?"

"Mm-hmm. As it happens, I did."

"And . . . ?" prodded Walt. A bite of impatience clipped the corners of her voice. A swift kick to her shin silenced her. Penelope, though eager, knew how to handle the likes of Harriet Greene, thank you very much.

When Penelope produced a crown and polished it with her gloved hand, the girl wet her lips. "The farmer was a Mr Andrews; however, my employer wasn't acquainted with his opponent. A newcomer or a visitor; he wasn't sure which."

Intentionally, Penelope's lips sank into a frown as she feigned an intention to return the coin to her reticule.

"The farmer's wound—" Harriet nearly reached out to snatch Penelope's wrist before regaining her senses. Composing herself, she clasped her hands at her waist. "It became infected, and he returned this morning. I overheard them talking." She stepped close enough to Penelope that her breath stirred the curls at the sleuth's shoulders. "The doctor recommended ginger and mint to his sister for the nausea she has in the mornings." The maid stepped back and winked. "If you catch my drift?"

A second crown appeared in Penelope's hand. Harriet tucked them into the pocket of her linen apron. Penelope tapped the side of her nose and winked before she bade her good day.

Alone in the passageway between the physician's home and a lodging house, with Walt stationed at the entrance, Penelope shed her talisman, restoring her eyebrows to their regular shape and shade. She tucked it into a containment pouch before dropping it into her reticule. Time, as fleeting as it was, did not permit her to return to her offices to change, so she undid her plain cotton dress and let it fall to the ground, revealing a finer muslin one underneath.

Walt chuckled. "Did you get what you needed?"

"Confirmed what I suspected is more like it." She folded the gown and placed it on the back step with a card that read, *For Harriet.*

They stepped into the lane and headed west. Streams of people, livestock, and carts bustled against one another, crisscrossing pell-mell in the gravel lane—a blur of taupes and russets smeared across the canvas of the square. Weaving through the chaos, they ducked under a wooden sign advertising a dowser.

Walt kept pace beside her. "Is it enough to clear your uncle?"

"No." She dodged a bedraggled maid walking a pair of yapping toy zilants. They yanked on their leads, begging for popcorn from a street vendor. "We cannot clear my uncle unless we are able to answer two questions."

As her friend was in dire straits, Walt humoured her blatant invitation to marvel at her cleverness. "And what questions might they be?"

"Why did the yeti counsel me not to head home on Sunday night?" As they turned the corner onto a side street, she halted abruptly in front of a freshly painted mural advertising dragon-drawn phaetons. The lift of an eyebrow made clear her intentions. "And what would motivate a future viscount to court a knight's daughter?"

# CHAPTER 27

## The Chapter with the Blushing Yeti

*"The gift of foresight is the least reliable of the crafts. Emotion oft clouds the seer's visions, making certainty a near impossibility."*

*A Study of Seers, 4th Edition*

Half an hour and three death-defying near misses later, a battered phaeton slowed as it narrowly missed the corner of Sable's dry-stone wall. The sapphire dragon entrusted with the carriage huffed as its occupants clutched their sides and one tumbled to the ground in hysterics.

"Lord, miss, have you never held a pair of reins before?"

Penelope straightened her bonnet before alighting. "Of course I have." She wiped a tear from her cheek. "Just not a pair with a dragon tied to the other end."

The sapphire, apparently not at all pleased with her steering, freed itself from its harness. Its lithe wings spanned the breadth of the roadway, reflecting the raw cotton clouds suspended in a vast sea of cornflower-blue sky. The gust from its wings as it took flight blew Walt's poke bonnet, adorned simply with a bouquet of tawny feathers, straight off her head. She scowled at the dragon, which landed in the field opposite to soak up the morning rays.

"That's why I don't like dragons," she began, picking bits of grass from her hat. "They—"

As Fate had a twisted sense of humour, it was at that moment that Toast landed with a thud behind her. Her recently righted bonnet fell from her head once more. With hands on her hips, her bottom lip pushed forward, and slits for eyes, she appraised the scaly intruder. "And who are you?"

"His name is Toast." Penelope scratched his chin, causing his lashes to flutter. Bright dewy buds peppered it like stubble. She grinned. Having claimed an (albeit fledgling) forest as his home had already begun to restore him to health. "He is now the guardian of the forest on my estate."

"Since when have you had a forest on your estate?" Walt jammed her bonnet onto her head, shielding her eyes from the sun that coyly peaked from behind the clouds.

"We always have, but it has long been in disrepair, which is why we needed a dragon to tend to it." Determined to ignore the darts her friend's eyes fired at Toast, she stepped between them. "Thank you for coming. I trust you received my message."

Toast bobbed his head.

"And you have called him?"

A good-natured roll of the eyes communicated, *Of course I have*. He tipped his horns towards Sable's cottage, which, if possible, had sunk deeper into the whirlpool of vines and shrubs that enveloped it. *Why are we here?*

"Why *are* we here?" Walt considered the house.

"We are here to meet with a yeti." Penelope brushed past her to the kissing gate. Its rusted hinges creaked like an opera singer with laryngitis shouting, *Intruders! Intruders!* As Toast could not wiggle through the gate, he leapt over it with care.

Walt appraised the thatch-roofed home. A wonky pair of chimneys teetered precariously, held in place by ivy and sheer tenacity. "Is this where he lives?"

"No." She hopped over a toppled garden gnome. {A clay one, of course. The living ones only visited on holidays to sample Sable's famed mead, but you did not hear that from me.} "I could not very well expect him to meet me by the third birch on the left, could I?"

Walt righted the gnome, patting it on its red polka-dot mushroom cap. "And how does he know to meet you at all?"

"Toast called him."

The ladies turned to discover that the forest dragon had tiptoed to a fishing net strung across two sentry Douglas firs like a hammock. Curled onto the net like a cat, he swished his tail, causing the trees to groan in protest.

Penelope did not miss the envious flash of green in Walt's eye. "Come, I must introduce you to Sable and secure a cup of tea while we wait."

No sooner had she spoken than Sable rounded the path from the back of the house. Though the morning light deepened the ravines that laughter and summer days had etched into her face, it transformed her hair into a halo of gossamer threads.

Her apprentice followed close behind, dressed in a cream dress and apron embroidered with flowers. A riverstone bound in copper wire hung from her neck. The two figures reminded Penelope of the primordial being Gaia and her granddaughter Eos, the goddess of the dawn. Or they would have, had not Sable glared at Walt as though she smelled of an outhouse.

The four women met at a literal crossroads cutting through the tangled garden. "Good morning, Sable." Penelope curtseyed. A pair of thief-thwarters guarding the path to the door nearly overturned her self-control. With no verbena leaves to rub under her nose, she bore the sensation as best she could. "This is my dear friend, Miss Walters."

She caught Walt curtseying in her periphery.

"Could we inconvenience you for a pot of tea while we wait for Mr Scott?" Her mouth curved of its own accord. "And a treat for our friend."

With a flourish of showmanship, Walt stepped away from Penelope, revealing Toast. The effect of seeing him swaying between two firs did not disappoint. Sable's stodgy veneer slipped when she beheld an elusive forest dragon lounging in her garden. She clapped her freckled hands over her mouth and bounded to him like a doe.

Her apprentice, not nearly as enthused, turned to Penelope. "Tea, then, miss, with honey. Yes?"

A raise of an eyebrow and a nod was all the permission she needed to disappear into the cottage.

With Walt by her side, Penelope meandered to the gazebo of roots, leaving Sable to fawn over Toast, who lapped up the attention. In the crow's nest of the rickety jollyboat overgrown with herbs reclined her confessor, the cat with a black spot over his eye. He nodded as she passed, formally though: careful not to betray their acquaintance.

Protected from the light by a canopy of wisteria and wildflowers, Walt shed her bonnet. "I thought *I* had kept strange company, but you, miss, you take the cake."

"You are not *so* very strange." A wry grin tugged at the corner of her mouth. Penelope selected the same seat she had before, a chair formed of roots and vines. She fluttered her eyelashes innocently. "And really, you ought not to say such things about yourself."

Whether it was her lips pressed into a line as straight as a reformed adulterer the morning after a church revival, or her scoff that was recorded three counties over, Penelope got the distinct impression that her friend did not find her quippy retorts as amusing as she did. A pity.

The sun rose in the sky, peering out from behind the clouds. Tease. Each handbreadth marked an hour. Tea had been drunk and pathways had been explored, yet Mr Scott had not appeared.

At some point, Walt had convinced Toast to wiggle over a foot to make room for her. Clearly, her qualms about dragons did not extend to those who had taken possession of the sole hammock.

As the day approached noon, Penelope began to pace: up and down, back and forth. The cells in her body transformed into fireflies trapped in a jar. They collided with her skin, causing stray tremors to erupt. It was in those moments that she would crush mint leaves or lavender flowers in her hand and inhale the fragrance, desperate to ground herself and remain rational.

The quiet moments between the torrents provided space for her to consider the nebulous circumstances surrounding Mr Montagu's death. Over and over again, she tested the web of theories that radiated outward from him like a stained-glass window. Her theory was sound: so sound she ventured to label it as fact.

Unable to remain still, she had taken to straightening the smooth river rocks lining the pathways. She was considering requesting gloves and an apron to weed the herb beds when Toast raised his head to stare into the forest. Penelope turned, hopeful. A minute passed before she spied the silhouette of a colossal man emerge from the wood.

"Good afternoon, Mr Scott," she called. The swarm of fireflies in her core darted every which way. "Thank you for coming."

"It is my pleasure." As it was a warm day, he wore a light linen shirt with cream breeches and a black chimney-shaped hat with a tapered crown and narrow brim. His honey-brown hair appeared to have been trimmed since they last met, perhaps in an effort to survive the oncoming summer months.

Before they delved into the matter at hand, niceties were observed. Sable was greeted as a friend, which Penelope had suspected, given the inventory of his medical kit. Toast's leg was inspected and was found to have miraculously mended of its own accord. (That or Sable had worked her magic, literally.)

It was Walt's greeting that Penelope found most entertaining. Though Mr Scott's shoulders were as broad as two gentlemen, and he towered over her by an arm's length, Walt lit her pipe, extended a hand, and said, "You're less hairy than I expected."

A hint of laughter in his voice assured Penelope that he was not offended. "Without a proper trim once a week, I look as shaggy as a woolly rhinoceros."

With greetings out of the way, Mr Scott gestured to a circuitous path that led away from prying ears, deeper into the chaos Sable called a garden. This path, though narrower, was free of talismans and wards, which suited Penelope and her nose.

"Mr Scott, no doubt you are curious why I asked Toast to call for you," Penelope began.

"When a pair of foxes delivered the message, I was intrigued." A true gentleman, he did not comment on the impropriety of the message. They had, after all, only met once. "It must be a matter of great import."

"It is." She turned to appraise him. There again, framed by wavy locks, were the kind eyes she had observed in the forest two nights prior. "As you may recall, you had counselled me not to return home the night we met."

"What is it about my words that give you pause?"

Though the troop of glowworms still whizzed from her head to her fingertips, she took care. "The cause."

As a seer, he could view jumbled flashes of the future, or so Penelope understood. What he could not ascertain were her thoughts or motivations.

He tilted his head. "I saw a body being dumped in a field."

"By whom?" She stepped forward.

"The vision was unclear, and I did not press into it."

"Please." Her hand reached across the space between them to rest on his arm. He studied it as though he had not been touched in some time. "My uncle—"

The mention of his name was like boiling water in an icy teapot. The reserved mask she wore fractured. Her fears bled through the hairline cracks—the quiver of her lip, the wetness on her lash-line.

Mr Scott knelt before her, eye to eye. "The night still hovered between evening and dawn when they left him."

"Who are they?" Her throat bobbed when she swallowed.

He shrugged. "A fine carriage drawn by two horses stopped at the edge of the lane. The coachman alighted. From the carriage, he lifted the body onto his shoulder and carried it to the field. A lady carried the pistol and his hat. She spat on the body."

"Have you seen them before?"

A wry chuckle escaped his lips. "I have few acquaintances."

Calm had regained a sufficient footing. She no longer begged, only hoped. "Is there nothing more you can tell me? No detail is too small."

He hung his head, the locks from his crown covering his eyes. "Nothing that can identify them. Only that I could sense the angel of death looming behind her."

Dear Mr Scott might have expected her to offer thanks or, perhaps, if he was fortunate, invite him to tea for his services and as recompense for crossing half of the forest. If he did, he was sorely disappointed.

No; rather than offer thanks or at least tip her head, Penelope looked as though she had encountered Medusa.

She did not move, nor speak, nor even blink. With her mouth pursed and her hands clasped, she stood like a statue. After some seconds, Mr Scott called to Walt.

In no rush, Walt meandered through the garden. Once she reached them, she scoffed. "'Tis nothing."

She waved a hand before her eyes. Still no response. "It's that mind of hers. When it gets to turnin' too fast, it can cause her to become all . . ." Walt's face went slack, mirroring her friend's.

Mr Scott rose cautiously, a bemused expression curling his lip. "Will she be alright?"

"In a moment." After several had passed, Walt shrugged. "Well, sometimes, she needs assistance."

"What kind of assis—?"

Assistance, in this case, came in the form of a shove, courtesy of Walt.

Ever the gentleman, despite his appearance, Mr Scott grabbed Penelope by the elbows to prevent her from falling on her derriere.

The effect was instantaneous. She had not even regained her footing before her body became animated once more. Her eyes snapped to his hands, which still clasped her arms. As if she were a flaming serpent, he released her and stepped back, muttering an apology. If hair could blush, his would have transformed into a ginger more brilliant than a harvest moon.

"Of course!" A quick curtsey and a smile sufficed as thanks before she turned on her heel and dashed down the path towards the gate. "It is absurd that I missed that before."

Walt followed in her wake. "Where are we off to?"

"First, to send a note." Penelope leapt across a patch of dandelions. "And second, to change."

"Into what?"

With a wicked grin, she said, "Gentlemen."

# CHAPTER 28

## The Chapter at the Gates of Hell (Proverbially)

"They say that the path to hell is paved with good intentions. Perhaps 'they' took the scenic route."

*A former dunner Dean Hall, Alderwood*

A lone gig weaved down a forest lane that evening. Though the moon reflected enough light to illuminate the path, the trees huddled together protectively, denying admittance. Their crowns swayed to the melody of the breeze. Rumours were murmured in moans to the undergrowth, which replied in a language of rustles and creaks. Hardwood roots clawed through the soil like outstretched fingers grasping at the earth.

The driver ought to have been scared witless; however, he was not. Firstly, his gig was towed by a dragon with scales the colour of a forest flush with the first breath of spring, keeping watch for predators with either two legs or four. Second, the driver was not, in fact, a man; he was a she, and not just any she.

"Remind me again why you are the wealthy gentleman, and I am your less influential friend," complained the short one of the pair in a tone better suited for satin and diamonds than a suit and boots polished to a high sheen.

"Because," cut in the driver, a chap of middling height, "you're shorter than I." If our reader has not put two and two together yet, the driver, dressed in a navy long-tailed coat and a silk hat, was none other than Walt, who continued, "Besides, I have the bearing of a landed gentleman."

"And I do not?" Incredulity dripped from every syllable of Penelope's voice.

"Nah, you glide like a lady, whereas I stride like a rake after a night at the—"

A tut from Penelope indicated that that was enough of that. No need to wax vulgar. And though she would rather be hung from her toenails in the town square than admit it, Walt could play a more convincing gentleman. With her pipe-smoking bravado, she was a natural.

The amber windows of a hunting lodge pierced through the murk, signalling their arrival. The brick facade with its rounded gables invited the wanderer in for a cup of tea or other vices if they were so inclined. Horses, dragons, and phaetons spilt out of the stable around the back, indicating a full house.

Penelope adjusted her cravat, thankful for the warmth it lent. "Do you remember the plan?"

"We have a plan?"

Toast scoffed. (Oh yes, the dragon was Toast, or per the plan which had been meticulously explained, "the brawn.")

"Are you serious?" Penelope checked her pitch, dropping it an octave for the benefit of a passing rider.

"Are you serious?"

Walt, who held the reins indelicately like a colonist (Ugh!), shook them for show. "When am I not?"

Penelope pressed her palm to her forehead; the coolness of the leather braced her against her ~~friend's~~ former friend's antics. "The chalkboard. The diagram. The bullet points."

"If you had wanted me to pay attention, you should have told me it was important."

"I did."

"But you neglected to mention that it was really, *really* important."

Limestone wedges, iridescent in the moonlight, lined the lane, directing them to the drive. Toast guided the gig to the front door, where a footman awaited. Since they stood at the gates of hell, their discussion on the definition of the word "important" would have to be postponed until another time.

Contrary to Penelope's expectations, a respectable footman appeared, attired in a luxurious burgundy coat. He bowed with due deference, awaiting the reins to guide Toast to the stables.

The arch of the forest dragon's brow conveyed, *Unlike others, I listened and shall be ready should you call.* Penelope winked at him before falling in a step behind Walt.

True to character, Walt sauntered like a man worth ten thousand a year. At the top of the stairs, she paused. "Remind me how this will save your uncle."

"Though I know who murdered Mr Montagu, I cannot prove it." Penelope stepped forward and tapped out a pattern of knocks and pauses. How she had learnt

215

it is a tale for another time; however, suffice it to say that directions and passwords to illicit establishments were one of the pieces of information she collected. "If, however, I can cast enough doubt in the minds of the jurors, they will have no choice to absolve him."

"Which leads us to . . . ?" A tap of heeled boots on the opposite side of the door cast a half-thrilled, half-panicked expression across Walt's moustached face. "Quick! Summarise! Go!"

Penelope drew a breath. "Short version: A future viscount destined to inherit a title and a lucrative estate would not marry a knight's daughter unless either: A. He had fallen madly in love."

"Unlikely." Walt adjusted her hat.

"Precisely. Mr Montagu was not in love with Miss Pilkington. Hence, he must have pursued her for another cause, which is B . . ." The lacquered wooden doors groaned open. "Capital."

A second footman greeted them with a bow before waving them inside. The hall that opened before them had the appearance of a fine estate playing dress-up as a country lodge. Panelled wood walls adorned with Irish elk and deer racks and plaques of mounted talons led to a fine, yet not ostentatious, staircase. Penelope caught a whiff of pipe tobacco blended with citrus-scented wood polish. The air was full of the hum of men's voices broken by bursts of laughter.

After they relinquished their outer coats, they strolled into the belly of the lodge. Penelope continued, "Until men inherit, they are permitted allowances. If Mr Montagu was a spendthrift, he exhausted his quickly, which led him to gambling." A dining room that had been transformed into a card room opened before them.

A dip of her chin signalled to Walt that they should enter the room. Pipe smoke and tension hung in the air, swirling above the heads of a dozen men gathered around two tables at either end of the room. Though the space reeked of wealth, Penelope sensed few charms were present. Perhaps gentlemen were less inclined to conceal their bald spots when ladies were not present to appreciate their efforts.

Hands in her pockets, Walt strode to the first to the table with Penelope at her side. "So I am to gather intelligence regarding Mr Montagu, am I?" she whispered.

A seedy man with a protruding chin threw a gold watch onto a table, disrupting glasses of brandy and coins with a clatter. Penelope scoffed. His tell—teeth raking across his bottom lip—shone like a blaring spotlight. And yet, a second man folded. Boars! Or bores; either one suits.

She leaned in to Walt. "The information need not even be intelligent." The man flipped his cards, a four, a seven, and a three; he had bluffed, obviously. "I wager the sum of the intellect present in this room, minus ourselves, of course, to be a negative number."

"Tsk. Tsk. Let us not be ungenerous." Walt strolled back into the hall. "It may equal zero."

The sight of herself in a gold-leaf mirror tugged a grin out from beneath Penelope's faux moustache. There reflected back at her were two gentlemen. Lean gents, yet gentlemen all the same.

Walt had worked her magic with the skill of a woman raised on the knee of a stage actress. Though Penelope did not need her breasts bound as her friend had, the addition of pads to her shoulders and chest created a rectangular silhouette.

A combination of burnt cork and ashes had been applied to create shadows. Artists' pigments lent sharpness to their features. Moustaches and wigs completed the look. So long as they did not venture into the light of day or remove their coats, they passed as gentlemen well enough.

"Remember, no stealing." Penelope eyed her friend knowingly as Walt wandered into a parlour turned mountain dragon's lair—papered black walls, gold chandeliers, and emerald drapes. With her pockets stuffed with more pounds than half the town made in a decade and the promise that she could keep her winnings, Walt indicated she wished to be dealt in.

Penelope lingered at the door, observing.

Though gambling has been designated as a game, it was, in fact, a dance. First, there was the shuffle, and then cards were dealt. The scraping of the stiff paper as cards slid across one another was the musicians tuning their instruments.

Second came the preening. Penelope leaned against the frame, amused. Like at a ball, the men fidgeted, fluttering their fingers and tapping their toes. The favoured ones loomed, petty tyrants of their table-sized domains. Each appraised the others, seeking a weakness.

Third came the dance. Bet. Play. Fold. Draw. Bet. Play. Call. Over and over again to a predictable rhythm.

Certain of her friend's abilities, Penelope perused the other ground-floor rooms, her eye roving for a ledger.

After a few minutes, she had sorted the employees of the gambling hell from the customers. The director, stationed near a high-stakes game of whist, was a gouty man with watery eyes. A flasher, planted to encourage speculation, shouted loudly, "Honestly, I cannot believe I have won as much as I have."

Waiters dressed in burgundy brushed from room to room, topping up drinks to keep the clientele tipsy. She even spied a puffer with grey hairs sprouting from his ears, swindling an earl as he complimented his ring. "Is that your family's coat of arms? The golden wyvern at the centre is exquisite."

Even after she had overheard titbits of gossip about the mayor and several peers of the realm, she had yet to spot the dunner. As he was responsible for collecting debts, he alone would have the ledger detailing Mr Montagu's misdeeds.

It was then that she spotted him: shoulders as broad as a barn barely contained by a bottle-green coat, the leatherbound book at his side. Fortunately, he was alone. Unfortunately, he was heading up the stairs.

She gained the first two steps. However, when a waiter darted by, Penelope flopped onto a stair. "Four hundred quid! What will my mum say?" she wailed in her deepest alto.

Sympathetic to her plight, the waiter approached and extended a glass of red liquid. "Try the table in the first room with the peaky-looking gentleman. He couldn't bluff to save his life." He winked before dashing back into the fray.

Provided with a ready prop, she climbed the stairs on wobbly legs. Tipsy men were often excused for being where they shouldn't. At the top of the stairs, she stumbled to the right, towards a carpeted hall lined with doors. Weaving side to side, she paused near one, then another, listening. Silence.

Discouraged, she nearly turned back before she noticed lamplight escaping through a crack at the final door. With care, she eased it open, prepared to collapse on her derriere should she be noticed. Thankfully, the butler had oiled the hinges recently. The door slid open noiselessly.

There stood the dunner with his back to the entrance. Amateur. As she did not wish to concuss an honest man who was simply trying to earn a living by swindling entitled gentlemen, Penelope opted to drug the man rather than whack him over the head.

Penelope willed her hands not to shake as she lowered her glass to the floor whilst removing a vial of dreamless sleep from her pocket. She flipped off the stopper with her thumb while tugging free her handkerchief. As the man was as wide as a wingback chair, she dowsed the cloth liberally.

Her tread was noiseless as she padded across the room. In a voice she had learnt after a fortnight as a maid in a bordello, Penelope pressed into the dunner's back, draping her arms over his shoulders, and murmured in his ear, "Do—Not—Move."

Excited by the prospect of an unsolicited tryst, the man chuckled—a grave error. By doing so, he had ex-haled, which would naturally necessitate a ready inhale.

Anticipating his reaction, Penelope pressed the dreamless-sleep-laced handkerchief against his mouth and nose. The poor dolt had not even time to struggle before he went as limp as a soggy stocking. With care, she lowered him to the floor.

"Sorry. It is nothing personal." She rolled him onto his side to prevent snoring. So that she would not be surprised, she slid the door closed and turned the key.

Once that was done, she crossed back to the desk. Papers and plates of half-eaten meals littered the surface. Though tempted (seriously tempted), she did not tidy before turning to the ledger. It did not take long for her to discover that Mr Montagu owed hundreds upon hundreds of pounds and had lost even more. Her body felt wired, as though she had drunk ten cups of tea.

Not wishing to push her luck, she closed the book and tucked it under her arm. A shout from downstairs, followed by the sound of shattering glass, quickened her pace. Penelope was about to step into the hall when she halted. Alone in the office, she permitted herself to grin.

There, hung beside the door, was a small burgundy coat with tails.

# CHAPTER 29

## The Chapter with the Mayhem

"That no person is to hit his Adversary when he
is down, or seize him by the ham, the breeches, or
any part below the waist: a man on his knees to be
reckoned down."

*Broughton's Rules 1743*

Ruckuses were as common in gambling hells as dashed
hopes. Hence Penelope did *not* sprint with trepidation
towards the sounds of an impending brawl downstairs.
Such disturbances were business as usual; no need to run.
Besides, Walt had behaved herself . . . probably.

However, once she had a moment to consider her
friend's proclivity for mayhem, she hastened her pace.
She descended the stairs in her newly acquired burgundy
coat and nodded to a passing footman as though they were
acquainted, trusting her "borrowed" uniform to shield her
from suspicion. The footman rolled his eyes as though to
say, *Gentlemen. Ugh!*

The hall was congested with the musk of hot (literally,
not metaphorically) men packed into one space, each
angling to peek inside one of the rooms. By stepping

on one or two toes, Penelope gained admittance to it. There, framed by the fireplace, was precisely what she expected—Walt nose to nose with a mountain disguising itself as a man.

"Are you insinuating, sir, that I, the son of a general, would cheat?" the man rumbled like Mount Vesuvius. Whispers flitted around the room. The crowd salivated at the scent of blood.

Penelope would have attempted to catch Walt's eye to signal that she had found the ledger and to indicate they could leave; however, as she knew her friend well, she stowed it behind an obliging plant instead and loosened her cravat.

With mock horror that could have impressed an audience at the Theatre Royal, Walt, still dressed in her coat-tails and sporting facial hair, pressed a fist to her bound chest. "Sir, I have insinuated nothing of the kind." She flashed Penelope a wicked grin. "I'm stating emphatically that you *are* a cheat . . ." Hands on her hips, she leaned in. ". . . and not a very good one at that."

As expected, the man, whose face resembled a tomato, cocked back his arm. Like most men, especially Alps-sized ones, he was sluggish, for he counted on his brawn rather than his brains to win his battles. That night was the last time he would make that mistake.

He let his arm fly; actually, fly is too generous a term. Let us try again. He let his arm sink through the air as though it were made of jelly. Walt smoothed her wig as she stepped out of the way.

It is a truth universally acknowledged that a man in possession of more muscle than intellect must be in want of a thorough thrashing by a woman half his size.

A guttural roar rolled across the room. The men nearest the ogre took a step back. Like a bull, he swung around and dived at his adversary only to miss again, tripping on the rug and colliding with the black-papered wall. Walt leaned against the table, entirely unaffected.

Penelope lifted her eyebrows. *Must we?*

The man pressed his palms to the wall to steady himself, his rounded shoulders rising with each inhalation.

*Come on; I never have any fun* was communicated by a half-shrug.

He spun with the speed of a tortoise, a double-barrelled pistol in his hand.

Penelope sighed. Amateur. When our heroine swung a perfectly executed roundhouse kick into his outstretched wrist, launching the gun across the room, the elation on Walt's face could have lit the town square. His gun skidded across the floor.

To say that all hell broke loose would be an understatement. A dozen men leapt into the fray, one landing a nicely delivered hook on the instigator's chin. Like a felled fir, he swayed, then collapsed onto the nearest table. Cards, drinks, guineas and pipes rained down on the bystanders, adding to the tumult. The directors and footmen, clearly professionals, scooped up the house's winnings and fled.

Sensing that Penelope was a threat, three men, who were either too inebriated or too foolish to behave in their own best interest, converged on her. A blow to a weak knee left the first writhing on the floor. A second was easily dodged and tossed headlong into the brick mantel.

Spittle flew out of the third man's mouth as he grabbed her by the collar and laughed. Poor man. He never saw her raised arm fall like a guillotine across his wrists, breaking his grip. With his hands trapped against her body, she winked just before her elbow sailed into his nose. Writhing in pain, he crawled from the room. Those nearest to her retreated to exchange blows with less capable foes.

The crack of splintering wood drew her attention. Walt, like the goddess she was, stood on the second table, a bottle of port in one hand and a man's cravat in the other, cackling. Even across the room, Penelope could hear the crunch of cartilage when Walt's knee connected with his face. She released him, but not before she tossed the bottle onto the hearth. Flames exploded outwards, licking the mantel.

Walt shouted above the din of fists colliding with flesh. "I prefer fighting in breeches, don't you?"

"Absolutely," Penelope replied, dodging a punch that sent a man tumbling pell-mell into the tea cart. She winced as a lovely teapot with blue artwork shattered. A pair of men who held one another by the shirts slid across the puddle like a pair of ice dancers. "Half the reason I have not handed most men of my acquaintance their tooshes on a platter is that I find it inconvenient fighting in a dress."

A tangle of sweat-soaked men rolled across the space between them. "Did I hear you right?" Walt dropped from the table into a crouch. A chair careered past her head before bursting into tinder against the wall. She leapt over a hunched man recovering from a punch to the gut, and landed beside Penelope. "Did you, a modern woman with stunning aim and worth God knows how many pounds, just say the word toosh?"

Penelope caught a flailing dagger by the handle as it flew towards her friend's face. She presented it to Walt, who aimed it expertly and lodged it between the eyes of a snooty portrait of a man in a white wig.

"Simply because—" She linked hands with Walt, clothes-lining a man. "—I observe the rules of propriety—" Walt dropped to one knee to avoid a sloppy swing of a cane. "—does not mean—" Penelope stepped onto her knee, using it as leverage to launch herself into an aerial kick, which levelled a man nearly as tall as Mr Scott. "—that I am in any way ridiculous."

After Penelope scooped up the ledger, the pair entered the hall. There at the door stood the dunner. Even at a distance of thirty paces, the veins throbbing on his forehead were evident. Two footmen, the director, and a few waiters had joined him. They listened as he gestured wildly.

Before the ladies could nip out the back, he turned. As you guessed, his eyes connected with the ledger.

Penelope shed her burgundy jacket. "Walt, I must know; why the spoons?"

Mayhem had set Walt ablaze—the rage of a thousand generations of women gleamed in her eye. She tore the wig from her head and shook out her coiled locks before casting it to the ground. Pure chaos consumed her. "If you must know, miss, I hope to collect enough to fashion a throne."

When the pair turned to the wall of testosterone blocking their exit, two of the men's knees buckled and one whimpered. Walt stepped forward but was halted when Penelope placed a hand on her chest. "Hold on."

Through her pursed lips, she emitted a whistle.

Walt swore. "What the—?"

The front doors swung open, whacking the walls, and an unlucky footman, with a resounding CRACK!

A wave of horror rolled down the hall at the sight of Toast. Smoke billowed from his nostrils as flames roiled in his closed mouth, radiating light through the gaps between his teeth.

"Oh, look, our transport." Walt waved at the forest dragon. "Come to rescue us, have you, you old scalywag?"

{Narrator's Note: She did indeed say scaly-wag, not scallywag. It is a pun.}

The flirt winked at her before letting loose a roar that reverberated in their chests. A hall mirror fell, shattering into dust.

The ladies strolled as though it were a Sunday afternoon through the pandemonium of men fleeing for their lives.

Upon reaching the doors, Penelope scratched Toast under the chin, eliciting a coo. "Shall we?" She gestured towards the exit.

Toast crouched so that they could climb aboard.

"No flying, you hear?" instructed Walt. A hint of anxiety was discernible in the edges of her voice.

If forest dragons could giggle, this one would have. He turned, took the steps in a single bound, and charged into the forest with the sounds of two women laughing trailing behind him.

# CHAPTER 30

## The Chapter with the Surprise

"'But he hasn't got anything on!' the whole town
cried out at last.

*The Emperor's New Clothes, Hans Christian Andersen*

Courtrooms were a mockery to the accused. They were
elegant in design only—cruelty parading as nobility. Like
the emperor with no clothes, the courts were blinded by
their pride, while the masses alone saw them as they truly
were, naked.

Penelope had risen early the morning of her uncle's
grand jury trial. They had ridden together, hands clasped,
exchanging words of comfort with one another. Though
the trial would not decide his guilt or innocence, it would
either absolve him or send him to a second trial, which
would decide his fate.

Due to her uncle's standing in the community, it had
been docketed for the early morning. They had been the
first to arrive, giving her time to observe.

The wood-panelled gallery was packed with those
seeking thrills at another's expense. They were the sort

who brought a picnic to a hanging and cheered when the life of the accused was not winked out at the drop of the trap door. To them, the twitching of a dying man's feet was a dance.

Though the room had been designed to represent justice and order with its fluted columns and ornate trim, it did not. It was a mockery. Stark white-washed brick reminded her of a mausoleum, not innocence. In her eyes, the judge's seat, wrapped in polished wood, resembled a coffin rather than the seat of justice.

When the constable indicated that the justice of the peace was about to enter the courtroom, she sat down on one of the benches reserved for the public. She studied the slope of her uncle's shoulders, his salt-and-pepper hair, and his perfectly starched collar.

The sight of it nearly broke her. Only twice in her lifetime had her uncle's valet successfully tamed his suit: the day of her parents' funeral and today.

That such a man could be accused of murder, a man who had treated even the urchin on the street with respect, robbed her of reason. They had not even permitted his valet to interpret, so he would face his fate blindly, relying upon their expressions to convey his fate.

Dread washed over her in waves: some lapping, others crashing, each threatening to crumble the walls of her self-possession. Society had taught her that, regardless of the circumstance, strength meant polite smiles and proper manners. To shed a tear—weakness. To openly weep—shameful. To admit that the cramping of her stomach stole her breath—worthy of censure. To wince at the ache of her chest, her back, her arms—absurd.

So, instead, Penelope sat straight as though someone had driven a fence post through her spine, her hands folded in her lap.

To her right sat her aunt in black, fitting for once. To her left was Mrs Stevenson, her alluring looks replaced by a hollowness reflected in Penelope's own heart. And far in the back sat Walt.

Across the aisle sat Mr Montagu's parents, his aunt and his uncle. His father, stone-faced, and his mother, a tempest of fury and grief, refused to turn toward Uncle Archie. Penelope longed to speak to them, to tell them what she knew. Would it assuage their loss? Likely not.

Before she looked away, Lady Montagu caught her gaze. The elder woman's eyes held not hatred but pity.

Lady Pilkington was seated further back, without her husband. Like most of the rabble, she behaved as though the proceedings were a spectacle, laughing with her neighbour as they waited. Though her titters and whispers painted a portrait of ease, Penelope noted the tremble of her hand as she squeezed her reticule.

Procedure was observed. Jurors were seated. The first witness was called: a farmer.

"On the morning of Monday the eighth of April, what did you observe?" began the prosecutor in his black robe and dusted wig.

The farmer, whose cheeks were flushed red from drink, looked to the jury. "'Twas just after sunrise when I came upon the stiff stretched out on the ground."

A couple of the jurors curled their lips at the disrespectful expression, their eyes taking in the mother of the deceased weeping into her handkerchief.

"That's when I spotted him." He nodded toward her uncle. "At the edge of the wood, hurrying towards his estate."

Over the mutterings of the gallery, Penelope noted a *tsk* from the back of the room—Walt. Though her assistant was blocked from her view by a dozen heads, she felt her support buoying her spirits. They had a plan if events went poorly—a spectacular plan involving explosives, several vials of illicit potions, and a coach waiting across the road.

After a few additional questions, her uncle's defence lawyer, Mr Steerforth, rose. Though the other defendants tried that day would not benefit from counsel, her uncle's wealth permitted him certain privileges. Mr Steerforth was a formidable man infamous for his tactics (or antics, according to many).

Mr Steerforth's black robe fell in an uninterrupted line from his sharp shoulders to his ankles. For show, he reviewed his notes before he turned on the farmer. A crooked grin flitted across his face. "Did you discover Mr Montagu in your own field?"

"No." He shook his head.

"No, indeed." He faced the jury. "It was on Mr Montagu's estate, several miles from your own, I might add, that you came across the deceased. Correct?" His tone was that of a man who already knew the answer.

Flustered, the farmer sputtered, "Yes, sir, I was up early making a delivery. I spotted it from the road."

"A road open to all, even the Prince Regent." Steerforth let the insinuation hang in the air. The farmer had discovered a body in another man's field not fifty paces from a well-travelled lane. Simply because her uncle had been in the vicinity did not make him a murderer, let alone a suspect. "Perhaps we ought to summon him as well?"

Members of the jury, the crowd, and even the constable sniggered. Uncle Archie peeked over his shoulder at Penelope, who hastily signed a summary of events while the judge attempted to restore order. Relief marginally smoothed the lines between her uncle's eyebrows.

Next, a physician was called to describe the state of Mr Montagu's body. His entire testimony could have been summarised in one sentence: "The cause of death was a single gunshot wound to the chest through the heart."

"Thrilling," spoke Mr Steerforth in a tone drier than the parson's wife's scones. "As his testimony can neither implicate nor exonerate my client, I have no questions at this time."

The next witness testified to her uncle's skill as a marksman. Since he was known throughout the region for his skill with a pistol, thanks to the annual charity picnics where gentlemen and ladies could display their abilities, the jury attended the witness's words. "The whole lot of 'em could shoot a man through the heart at thirty paces, if not more."

Though his words were meant as a compliment, she wished that, given the circumstances, he had not waxed so eloquently about their shared skill.

While the next witness was sworn in, she noticed a shift in the jury. Two men who had appeared more friendly to her uncle's plight began to avoid looking in his direction.

The final witness presented by the prosecution was a wealthy gentleman with a curled moustache who had been present at Viscount Montagu's estate that fateful night. He wore a fine coat and had the bearing of a gentleman, unlike her uncle, who, despite his best efforts, resembled the village loon playing dress-up rather than the landed gentry he was.

"Mr Sedgewick's valet indicated that his master had accused Mr Montagu of palming cards." Like most men of means, he spoke with authority, as though one would be a ninny to question his words.

"And how did Mr Montagu react to this accusation?" asked the prosecutor.

The room leaned forward.

"Poorly. He called him an addled simpleton." He paused, his jaw rigid, lip curled. "Then he spat in his face."

Though she did not turn her head, she noted the knuckles of Mrs Stevenson's hands blanch as she curled her hands into fists. As for Aunt Josephine, she could have set the courtroom ablaze with the fury veiled behind her blue eyes.

When asked how her uncle responded, the witness toyed with his moustache, then replied, "Though Mr Sedgewick did not speak, he gestured to his man. While I did not comprehend, he appeared to be livid."

Two of the jurors gave one another a knowing look. So then it would come down to this. Could a jury of men be swayed to believe that her uncle harboured a grudge or not? The cramping in Penelope's belly intensified.

When it came time for Mr Steerforth to question the gentleman, he approached him and placed the ledger on the stand with a thump. "Sir, this is the ledger from the Hunting Lodge, a local gambling hall, as evidenced by the inscription on the inside of the cover. Could you turn to the first page and find Mr Montagu's name towards the bottom?"

Wary, the gentleman flipped to the page and drew his finger down the lines. The moment his eyes read the sum next to Mr Montagu's name, an understanding dawned in them.

"Read aloud the sum Mr Montagu owed, if you would be so kind," the defence lawyer instructed.

The man's protruding Adam's apple bobbed when he swallowed. "One hundred and twenty-one pounds."

A pause permitted his words to fester. The effect on the jury was mixed. While one or two gave the information the weight it deserved, at least half appeared unimpressed or, worse, disinterested.

While the lawyer continued to have the witness read off sums attached to Mr Montagu's name, Penelope hazarded a glance at Mrs Stevenson. She, too, understood. Her mouth drooped. Her eyes flicked to Uncle Archie, Aunt Josephine, and then to Penelope. When she met her young friend's gaze, they softened for an instant before snapping away.

Minutes later, the witness was excused, having read aloud debts totalling several hundreds of pounds. As Mr Steerforth returned to his seat, Penelope perceived Mrs Stevenson dip her chin.

When the time came for the defence to call its witnesses, Uncle Archie's lawyer rose and called out, "I would like to call Mrs Abigail Stevenson to the stand."

A current coursed through the room, triggering a chain of whispers and speculation. Uncle Archie, aware of the hubbub but not its source, turned to seek an explanation. One came in the form of Mrs Stevenson standing, smoothing her airy blue dress, and crossing to the witness stand.

His expression was not one of shock but dismay. Her aunt looked at her, puzzled. Before the justice of the peace had sworn in her friend, Penelope understood.

After her name was given for the record, Mr Steerforth asked, "Mrs Stevenson, have you evidence to offer in this matter?"

She lifted her chin, unabashed, and answered both aloud and in sign, "I have."

"Of what nature?"

"Mr Sedgewick could not have committed the crime of which he has been accused." She stared at one juror after the other, allowing her words to hang in the air. "For, on the evening of Sunday until after sunrise the next day, Archibald—" A gasp echoed from the back of the room. "—was with me."

It was Walt's characteristic laughter that rang out the loudest, even above the uproar that descended upon the court. Without meaning to, Penelope began to giggle uncontrollably. To her surprise, Aunt Josephine's shoulders bounced as she failed to contain a chuckle.

Her aunt waved her near and whispered, "Shows us how clever we are. Never once did I suspect they harboured anything more than mutual admiration and friendship for one another." It would be minutes before her shoulders would return to their natural rigid posture once more.

Of course: it had been with Mrs Stevenson her uncle had been secretly corresponding for over a decade. And though the lady brandished brazenness like a new bonnet, the look on her uncle's face convinced her that their tryst had never ventured beyond the pages of their letters.

Penelope observed an alteration in the faces of the jurors. Doubt was displaced by relief; the weight that had been pressing upon her chest lifted. And though it pained her to observe Mr Montagu's family huddled in their own private grief, she could not help but feel elated.

Naturally, the case was dismissed—it would not go before the Court of Assizes.

Though the Montagus rushed to their carriages, the rest of the town lingered outside the courthouse to congratulate the Sedgewicks. There were grins and winks aplenty as their neighbours wondered how a man who had never worn a pressed shirt a day in his life could capture the affection of the likes of Mrs Stevenson.

After shaking hands with half of the town and hugging her uncle before he stepped into his carriage, Penelope spied Walt leaning against the getaway gig.

"Need a ride?" Walt asked when she approached.

"As a matter of fact, I do." She climbed into the passenger's seat. "It is time to reveal the whereabouts of Miss Pilkington at last."

# CHAPTER 31

## The Chapter with Wild Roses

"Thief-thwarters are rubbish. If you have a home
in need of protecting, get yourself a cat and pistol,
in that order."

*Sable Kiplinger, resident of Gloucestershire*

When Prudence Clearwater (that is, Penelope in disguise)
knocked at the arched door whose porthole window had
doubtlessly been ripped from the hull of a schooner left
to rot on the floor of the ocean, she did not expect a sea
captain to answer the door. And one did not.

As the hinges whined in protest, a familiar scowl
appeared—Sable. "What'd you want?"

Penelope was tempted to chuckle. It was comforting
to know that the nurturer was not an elitist and greeted
both the wealthy and working class with an equal measure
of hostility. "My name is Prudence Clearwater, and my
employer has been hired to discover the whereabouts of a
Miss Rose Pilkington."

Though her lined mouth may have said, "Who?" her
eyes shouted, "Crap, crap, crap!"

As women of Sable's calibre were known for possessing more tenacity than a pack of besotted suitors, Penelope decided to apply directly to Miss Pilkington. "Miss Pilkington, I mean you no harm. Please, come to the door."

A shuffling from within reassured her. In the West Country accent she adopted when playing Miss Clearwater, she spoke again, more gently and with care. "Please. I wish to help."

"Let her in, Sable." A set of well-trimmed nails curled around the door. It swung open to reveal Rose Pilkington, or Sable's apprentice, without the riverstone charm to disguise her natural refinement.

Penelope stepped inside. The protectiveness lurking behind Sable's crystal eyes assured her that the nurturer would relish the prospect of burying her in the back garden. After all, bodies were excellent fertilisers. She shrank under the woman's gaze in hopes of relieving her concern.

When Rose led her to the sitting room, Penelope felt more at ease. If they had had ill intentions, they would have led her to the kitchen or even the root cellar. Bloodstains were a beast to scrub out of upholstery.

As she passed through the keyhole archway leading to the sitting room, she was tempted to chuckle. The room's overstuffed couch and mounds of embroidered pillows perfectly mirrored the chaos of the garden. Though it was well kept, plants grew from every teapot, every vase, and even a mismatched boot. Their leaves bent towards the picture window overlooking the garden.

Even the walls reflected Sable's love for the natural world. Every spare inch of wallpaper and plaster had been covered with paintings of fields, forests, and mountains.

Since the vertical spaces had been claimed, artwork had been hung on the ceiling as well.

Tea was not offered when they were seated. This was, after all, a touchy call and not one to be extended by a tea service.

Miss Pilkington, her hair returned to its usual shade and her eyes more round, folded her hands in her lap and waited. Sable settled next to her protectively. A hand remained in her apron pocket, grasping a potion or weapon, no doubt.

Eager not to give her hostess a cause to withdraw whatever lay hidden within the cotton folds, Penelope began. "Did you witness Grace's death, or did you merely happen upon her?"

The girl's bright eyes grew wide. A hint of admiration danced at their corners. Her whereabouts had been quite the mystery and, naturally, she was impressed. "I saw him flee, or thought I had. When I entered the room and discovered her dead, I put two and two together."

Penelope nodded, having surmised as much. "Of course. My employer also deduced that you prepared the tea yourself." Her old friend, the cat with the eyepatch-shaped spot over his eye, loped into the room. He sniffed the air around her.

"Yes, I did." Rose blinked several times. "How did he know?"

A wren with breast feathers the colour of honeycomb flew through the window, providing a welcome distraction. It landed on Sable's shoulder, nipping at her white fichu tucked into the neckline of her dress. When she turned to collect a music box filled with seeds, Penelope laid her open reticule on the rug, careful to tip the catnip onto the carpet. The whiskered rogue swooped it up and scurried under the wingback chair before anyone was the wiser.

The bird, having collected a beak full of seeds, flitted to a nest tucked between two books on the mantel.

"The sugar bowl."

In unison, both Sable and Rose tilted their heads to one side like a zilant.

"My employer informs me that you neglected to add the sugar bowl to the tray."

Miss Pilkington's hands flew to her mouth as she rocked back and giggled. "I must have. Your employer is clever, is he not?"

Though Penelope wished to correct the girl about the sex of her employer, she did not. The fewer people who knew of Patience Jones and Prudence Clearwater, or that their employer was a she, the better. "Yes, he is."

Sable grabbed a pink apple twice the size of one grown without the aid of a nurturer and bit into it. "My question is, how did your employer know she had taken refuge here?" Bits of juice and fruit fell from her mouth.

Penelope did not curl her lip, not even a little, though she desperately wanted to. To prevent herself from offering a handkerchief, she locked eyes with Rose. "From what he has told me, it was a combination of logic and a bit of footwork that led him to discover your whereabouts."

The rise of one of Sable's bushy eyebrows indicated that her hostess found her explanation lacking.

Penelope drew a breath before she plunged in, squashing the giddiness threatening to expose itself in her expression. "First, your diary mentioned the yeti on several occasions, but not a beau. This led my employer to suspect that you frequently wandered the wood and may have come across one of its two-legged inhabitants.

"There were precisely two captains whose time ashore could have coincided with your trip to Cardiff." She rose to pace the bare hardwood floor, which creaked with each step. At each end of the room, she paused for dramatic effect. "One has recently married. And the other . . ." *good ole Franny* ". . . is in London, visiting his aunt."

She turned to face her. "Furthermore, not a single inn, tavern, or . . ." *bordello* ". . . business entertained a captain Friday or Saturday last. Given this information, my employer deduced that you were not engaged and had not eloped."

Sable nodded, impressed. "Not bad, not bad. But how'd he discover she'd hidden here?"

This bit was a tad tricky. It was at her meeting yesterday with Mr Scott that she had put it all together. Rose had offered honey with her tea without her asking, an unconventional preference, one that only an acquaintance would know.

Since she could not divulge that she had visited the house before, she lied. "After the housekeeper blabbed that she had spotted Miss Pilkington escaping into the woods, he sent a couple of lads to poke around the edges of the forest."

As she bent first to sit and then to right her reticule, she steadied herself. Sable had more wards and talismans than half of the manors in the county. Would she believe that a lad had slipped through unnoticed?

The woman shrugged. "Damn thwarters. Not worth ground they're staked to, if you ask my opinion."

Apparently, she would.

Penelope, unable to leave one string loose, asked, "May I ask, why did you flee? Why not simply alert the household?"

"I was scared." Miss Pilkington's hands wrung her apron. She looked to Sable and then to Penelope, begging them to understand. They did. Though a woman of one and twenty was of age, Rose was still a girl at heart. "I had not been too keen on marrying Mr Montagu, but as I was eager to have a home of my own, I welcomed his attentions."

Regret played across her face in the glassiness of her eyes and the curve of her lip. "My home . . ." Her voice cracked. Sable took her hand. "My home is not a happy one. I could prove nothing, and I feared my parents would expect me to proceed with the courtship to protect their standing."

The elder woman's expression reflected the quiet anger Penelope felt. Words, in this circumstance, felt hollow, so she nodded, conveying her sympathies with a look.

"So I wrote a note to my mother and slipped it under her door." Rose smoothed her light linen dress. "A second, to be delivered by my maid, was sent to the housekeeper."

"For the basket?" Penelope asked.

She tipped her chin. "Then I fled to . . ."

*Mr Scott.*

". . . the woods, to seek the aid of a friend. He brought me here, to Sable, promising that she could help."

242

The kindness in Sable's eyes convinced Penelope that the healer who sat before her tended to things more delicate than flowers and mended wounds that ran deeper than broken bones.

A breeze trickled into the room, stirring the curtains, carrying with it a question.

The seeds of a plan began to germinate in Penelope's mind—a plan she hoped would free Rose in more ways than one. "As you may have heard, Mr Montagu has been killed."

"We had nothing—" began Sable.

"I know." She leaned in. "And your mother, though she is convinced you have eloped, has circulated that you are visiting a cousin."

The girl's expression told her that Rose had not heard as much. Good: she had cut all ties with the household.

"If you would not mind indulging in a bit more subterfuge, I have a plan that could permit you to continue living here or elsewhere, should you wish it."

Rose moved to the edge of her seat. "Tell me. What must I do?"

Penelope did not conceal the mischievous satisfaction she felt rising in her chest. "How do you feel about becoming a mama?"

A half hour and a cup of tea later, Penelope emerged. A quarter of a mile up the road waited Walt, napping under a tree.

"Oh good, you're alive," Walt called, her eyes still closed.

"Had you thought otherwise?" Penelope's charm and hat were stowed in her bag. A finer bonnet awaited her on the seat of the gig.

Walt pushed herself up. "Nah, though if any woman could beat you, I would guess that nurturer would be equal to the task."

Penelope chuckled. She was not wrong.

One at a time, the ladies climbed into the gig.

"Where are we off to next?"

In a tone reserved for ladies discussing cross-stitch patterns, Penelope shook the reins and answered, "To confront Mr Montagu's executioner."

# CHAPTER 32

## The Chapter with the Executioner

"I would rather face Napoleon's fleets than cross
paths with a vexed woman."

*Regent of the United Kingdom of
Great Britain and Ireland*

"Which did you discover first?" Penelope rested her teacup
on her lap. Tea with honey had been offered on this call.

Across from her, with floral embroidered pillows at
either elbow and a teacup and saucer balanced on her
knee, sat Mr Montagu's killer, clad in cream muslin and
sporting a sage ribbon in her hair.

"Discover what, my dear?"

"That your nephew killed Grace Sullivan . . ." She
paused for dramatic effect, of course. All of the best
sleuths do. ". . . or that you were ill."

"Oh, you are clever." Admiration curled the corners
of Lady Montagu's angular lips. It enlivened her bold
features, transfiguring their plainness into beauty. "In fact,
you may be the most brilliant Sedgewick in a century."

With the filtered sun shining on her face, the effects of her illness were evident: the bluish tint circling her lips and the slight tremble whenever she extended her hand.

In light of her illness, it was no wonder she had applied such bold redecoration to the drawing room in which they sat. The midnight walls, the vibrant flowers, and the constellations of gold overhead reflected her stalwart spirit.

As the cat was out of the bag, Lady Montagu lifted her cup to her lips, not attempting to conceal the shake. Tea sloshed wildly from one side to the other, falling to the napkin in her lap.

She reclined against the pillows, a queen with a whimsical grin playing at the corners of her mouth. "As to my illness, it was the scarlet fever last autumn. The infection wreaked havoc, weakening my heart."

Penelope pressed her lips together. Despite the fact that the lady had shot her own nephew, she pitied her. "How long?"

"Not long. I doubt I shall survive the spring. It is just as well . . ." The lady shrugged. "I loathe the winters."

They remained quiet for some moments, letting the weight of her words hang between them. Lady Montagu, even with her wealth and title, would die, as would they all. Death pardoned no one.

The Viscountess drew a deep breath, then turned to her guest once more. "Regarding the other discovery: though I had known of his philandering, his debts, and his wild living for years, I only learnt he was a murderer three evenings ago."

Penelope had hazarded as much. At her last call, while the viscountess had not seemed especially fond of her nephew, she had not appeared to harbour substantial ill will towards him. She patted the corner of her lips with a crisp handkerchief. "May I enquire how you discovered it?"

"I did not discover it so much as he confessed it." She laughed wryly.

Since their cups, a Delft blue design depicting a provincial scene, were empty, Penelope refilled them, adding sugar to her hostess's cup and honey to hers. She then settled back into her wingback chair and waited for the Viscountess to continue.

"Sometimes I find it difficult to sleep in my bed. It is the mattress—too soft. On such nights, my husband will carry me down the stairs so that I may sleep here." She patted the cushion of the canapé. "It is perfection."

After a sip to wet her dry lips, she continued, "That evening, my nephew wandered in drunk, senseless and barely able to stand, let alone think. He plopped down at the piano." Her hand lifted in the direction of the fine instrument housed in the corner of the room. A breeze caught the ceiling-height orchid curtains, fanning them.

When Penelope turned to Lady Montagu once more, disgust had settled onto her brow. "The blackguard sat there, senseless of my presence, pounding away. Moaning, 'I killed her. I didn't mean to. It was an accident. My Grace. My love.'" She spat the words like acid. "He had no right to call her his love after what he had done."

To prevent herself from spilling how precisely she had learned of Mr Montagu's love affair with Grace, Penelope drained her cup and then refilled it.

Lady Montagu continued, "He did not even notice me lying here, listening. The longer it went on, the more ill it

247

made me." She shook her head. "As I could not count on men to dispense justice, especially as I, the sole witness to his confession, might not survive until trial, I waited.

"When he had collapsed against the piano, I shot him. He would not disgrace the name of Montagu ever again." She leaned forward to fetch a cake with a white icing and lemon drizzle. "Convincing my steward to assist with the disposal of the body was simple enough. A few tears and a story about mistaking him for an intruder was all it took. His family has served ours for a century; covering up our connection with Mr Montagu's death was as much in his best interest as ours."

Though Penelope understood her, one question unsettled her still. She reflected on the unsigned letter she had sent to the Viscountess via a reliable errand boy two days prior. It had contained four words: *Confess or be exposed.* "I understand. What you were intending to do if my uncle—?"

"Ah, yes. Your note. Quite melodramatic." She grinned. "If your uncle's case had been sent to trial, I intended to confess, even before your note arrived."

Lady Montagu continued, "As it stands, I have entrusted letters to my lawyer to be delivered upon my death—to my husband and to his nephew's parents. Of course, I have softened the story, for their sakes."

They looked out of the window at the pristine gardens, the lawn stretching to the wood, each wondering what would come next. A pair of grey squirrels chased one another across the garden. A lake dragon crested in the pond, its back slicing through the water. Life persisted.

Not wishing to add another burden but knowing she must, Penelope spoke, her voice laced with sympathy.

"A Mr Andrews, a farmer, duelled with Mr Montagu last week."

Lady Montagu studied her, not yet certain of the connection.

"He has a sister whom I suspect is with child."

"I see." Understanding dawned across Lady Montagu's face. "I shall arrange for the child to be provided for."

After one's guest accuses one of murder and one confesses to the crime, it may be a bit difficult to return to discussing bonnets and the weather. However, as Lady Montagu was a proper English viscountess, she soldiered through the quagmire of discomfort and smiled pleasantly. "And where do we go from here?"

Penelope sipped her tea, considering. "Are you asking whether I intend to tell others?"

Lady Montagu dipped her chin.

"No, I do not." She shook her head. "No. Justice has been served for Grace and for the others he used for his own pleasure. I think, in this instance, it is better to let sleeping dragons lie."

Calm draped itself over the lady's shoulders like a quilt, soothing her expression. She raised her cup and bowed her head. "As I said, the cleverest Sedgewick in a century."

# CHAPTER 33

## The Last Chapter

"Parting is such sweet sorrow that I shall say
goodnight till it be morrow."

*Shakespeare, Romeo and Juliet*

May had wrought scant changes to Birch Hallow and its inhabitants. To celebrate the good weather and the fact that no one had been hanged the month prior, on the first day of the month, the family, along with Mrs Stevenson, traipsed into their woods to enjoy a picnic.

A hand cart filled to the brim with blankets, pillows, and dishes was wheeled by Uncle Archie. Cerberus was perched atop a pillow, swaying precariously with each divot or bump. Each lady carried a kettle or a pot. Ambrose bounced at their heels. A perfect afternoon, or so Penelope had advertised when she had persuaded her aunt and uncle to clear their schedules.

At the edge of the lawn awaited their host, Toast.

"Good afternoon, sir," called Penelope.

The forest dragon, ever the gentleman, bowed. When he grinned, a few of his fangs peeked out, adding even more charm to his appearance. They fell into step with one another, leaving the rest of their party to admire the fruit of Toast's efforts.

In the span of a few weeks' time, Toast, with the help of Sable and a dozen other well-paid nurturers, had reclaimed the wood from the bog it had become when the path of a nearby river had been altered. The puddles had dried, permitting ferns and shrubs to thrive.

"My compliments." Penelope scratched him under his chin. "Mr Scott informed me that the rabbits and moles he persuaded to relocate to your forest are pleased with their new home."

*Of course they are pleased. This is not my first forest, after all,* was communicated in a shrug. He then directed her with a nod towards a glen near the middle of the wilderness.

"And the fields are coming along nicely. The firs are already to my chin. By the autumn, I expect them to pass even Mr Scott's height."

Toast's beard of moss and clover flushed the colours of autumn—in other words, he blushed. The compliments were well deserved. In a few years' time, their corner of the world would become the loveliest wood in all of the western counties. Of that, Penelope was certain.

Mother Nature, as thanks, had sped along Toast's recovery. Every other day, Penelope had noted new sprouts or buds pushing through the cracks between his scales. And though it might take years for his horns to heal (if ever), ivy had wound itself around the antler-like rack, concealing the carvings. She had yet to persuade him to divulge the identity of his enslaver, but one day . . .

Ambrose, who had come to view Toast as an elder sibling, hopped next to him, begging him to play catch with a pine cone. The ever-patient dragon obliged.

Alone, she slowed her pace to match her aunt's.

"Ghastly." Her aunt's nose crinkled. She supported the copper kettle with both hands, taking care not to spill a drop on her coal-black gown.

Penelope considered her aunt, confused.

Aunt Josephine jutted her chin towards her brother and Mrs Stevenson, who were walking an arm's length apart and behaving respectably. "I do not know what is worse, that he misses dinner once a week or that she joins us for breakfast on occasion."

"Personally, I find breakfasts with Mrs Stevenson diverting." And she did.

The unspoken sentiments and furtive glances were delicious. Ever since Mrs Stevenson's confession in court, their relationship had blossomed into . . . Well, no one exactly knew. Letters were still exchanged, though, by her uncle's own hand. And he had been absent for dinner twice, though he had reappeared by breakfast the next morning as rumpled as ever.

Last Tuesday, Penelope had been so bold as to lean into Mrs Stevenson and ask her to spill the beans: How had it all come to pass? Why the locked box?

After Mrs Stevenson had thrown back her head and laughed, her luscious coral lips pursed, suppressing a grin. "It began quite innocently. Ten years ago, your uncle, on a whim, placed the box in the forest, containing an anonymous letter."

Having finished buttering his bread, her uncle added, "I checked it from time to time until, one day, I discovered a reply bearing no signature." A blush shaded his face. Overcome with shyness, he turned his attention to Cerberus, permitting the ladies to continue.

"At first, neither of us knew with whom we corresponded." Mrs Stevenson continued, a tenderness blanketing her handsome features. "As I had recently lost my husband, I found solace in your uncle's words. It was a bright spot in the midst of my despair. After a couple of years, I put two and two together, but I had no desire to disturb the little world of words we had created."

"So then you have written to one another anonymously this entire time?"

"Even still." Mrs Stevenson's eyes crinkled at the corners when Cerberus leapt into Uncle Archie's lap to bathe his face in kisses. "We never signed our names. But do not tell your aunt. It is far more delightful to watch her squirm at the thought of her brother and dearest friend embroiled in a torrid affair."

At those words, Penelope impersonated a spring, spewing tea across her skirt.

It was the second dress tea had stained that month. Weeks prior, she had suffered Lady Pilkington's own impression of a fountain when she had sat across from her, dressed as Prudence Clearwater, and had revealed that her daughter was unmarried and with child. And while the first half of her statement was true, the second was not. Out of the goodness of her heart, Miss Clearwater had consented to be a courier, exchanging letters between the mother and daughter, delivering a monthly allowance, and ensuring Rose was well looked after. The arrangement would not last forever, but it sufficed for now.

And it was the present that Penelope ought to return to. A whisper of wind stirred her sage muslin gown as she followed Toast deeper into the forest. After ducking under an archway of roots and moss, a verdant meadow opened before them—a fairyland.

The party meandered through the tall grasses interlaced with wildflowers. The columbines' bell-shaped petals twirled like ladies in a ballroom. Fallen logs lay in perfectly imperfect squares, ideal for fireside chats. Even a stream had been invited to wind through the field, lending its voice to the chirp of grasshoppers and the melodies of songbirds. It was paradise.

An obliging tree was their canopy, a stump their table. Pillows and blankets were arranged, water was boiled over a modest fire, care of Toast, and tea was served.

While the members of the party without wings or scales lounged in the shade, reading, talking, and most definitely not linking little fingers under a pillow, the rest of the party chased butterflies and climbed trees.

When Penelope lay back, her hands behind her head, one word came to mind—idyllic. And though she felt Walt's absence, neither of them was prepared for her to become an acquaintance to her aunt or uncle. For Walt, the only ties she wished for belonged to laces and bows. And for Penelope, by revealing her gifts to her friend, she had reached her honesty quota for the year, thank you very much.

Instead, Penelope had provided her with funds sufficient for a fortnight on the coast. Tucked into a bag specifically purchased for the voyage was a silver spoon, one from her own set, and a note.

*Thank you for your help.*
*Your Friend, P*

To which Walt responded, "Think nothing of it, miss. After all, the best friendships always include a spot of mayhem."

And so our cosy story comes to a close; that is, until another poor sod is maimed or disappears . . . or becomes a field dragon's afternoon tea.

Probably best, then, to check back shortly, for the chaos that surrounds our cast of characters will doubtlessly whip itself into a frenzied whirlpool soon enough.

# THE END
(Sort of)

# MEET the author

K. Starling creates stories set in a reimagined Regency era, overflowing with dragons, intrigue, and magic.

When she is not writing witty female heroines or delicious villains, she will hit the trail with her family or the open road in her tent. And though she does not have a pet, her kids have a menagerie of dinosaurs, stuffies, monsters, and dragons.

An avid reader, she has long nurtured a dream of penning a novel in her name. After twenty years of writing articles, novels, and blogs for organizations and clients, K. Starling is thrilled to publish her debut novel Talismans, Teapots, and Trysts this summer.

FIND HER ON. . .
Instagram & Threads: @authorkstarling
Website: authorkstarling.com

Milton Keynes UK
Ingram Content Group UK Ltd.
UKHW041904180724
445674UK00005B/224

9 798990 646605